MW00879944

Adventures Of A Graveyard Girl

MILDA HARRIS

Books by Milda Harris:
Adventures in Funeral Crashing (#1)
Adventures of a Graveyard Girl (#2)
Adventures in Murder Chasing (#3)
The New Girl Who Found A Dead Body
Connected (A Paranormal Romance)
Doppelganger (#1)
Doppelganger 2: On the Run (#2)

Copyright © 2012 by Milda Harris
All rights reserved.
ISBN: 1480003441
ISBN-13: 978-1480003446
Cover Art by Brett Gilbert Copyright © 2012

DEDICATION

To anyone who has a dream, get up and follow it!

CONTENTS

ACKNOWLEDGEMENTS

Thank you to my editor, Lauren Cramer, for all of your proofreading, editing, and funny comments. And, thank you to Brett Gilbert, for your always amazing artwork and for being an equally amazing husband.

CHAPTER 1
HOMECOMING DANCING

I was going to the Homecoming Dance with Ethan Ripley, the most popular guy in school, even though I was the weird girl. Could life get any better? No, I didn't think so, at least not in the foreseeable future.

Wow, I couldn't believe how hot Ethan looked dressed up in a suit and tie. His tie was a bright blue and it made his eyes stand out even more than normal. I was already dying to run my hands through his dark, wavy hair. It was funny, I'd never really thought much past how amazing he already looked in just jeans and a T-shirt, but there was something about a suit and tie that made my stomach do loops. I just never knew that until this very moment. That was probably because this was my first time being on a date to a dance with a guy I thought was really hot already. Well, Ethan was actually my first date to a dance ever.

I thought I looked pretty good too, at least that's what I gathered from the double take Ethan did when he saw me as I answered the front door when he arrived to pick me up. I was wearing a silvery blue dress with spaghetti straps. It was just past the knee and flowing, yet clingy in all the right places. My shoes were these really amazing silver sandal heels and because I had a tendency toward the clumsy and always felt rickety in heels, I had practiced in them, so I wouldn't fall or, simply, look like an idiot walking in them. I had even gone through the trouble to get my hair done at a salon, so it was up in a twist with curls and I had a couple tendrils of hair framing my face. When I looked in the mirror, it was a little scary. It almost didn't look like me, especially after I put on my make-up. I almost wished I had gone to a makeup counter and had that done too. Then I really would have wowed Ethan. Next dance. It was hard to believe that I was already thinking about a next dance with Ethan! I couldn't help it. He was just so amazing. I was gushy about him, I'd admit to that. Well, to myself at least. He didn't need to know. I hoped that he was at least half as gushy about me. I mean, I thought I looked pretty great and I wouldn't normally be saying that.

Nobody would have known that I was in the hospital only a week ago. Yeah, that's right, the hospital and I did have a scar, but it was covered up as best as I could with make-up. I was shot while solving Ethan's half sister's murder case. The upside was that for two whole days afterward, Ethan stayed by my side almost around the clock. It wasn't that serious of a wound, thank goodness, but it was still nice of Ethan to stay with me. Ethan even brought me a couple peanut butter banana milkshakes from my favorite coffee shop, Wired. I love peanut butter banana milkshakes so that was super awesome of him. They are heaven on earth! He didn't need to do that either. Just having him to talk to and pass the time with would have been enough. Well, that and the kissing.

I mean, even though I was out sick from school and really had gotten injured, it had been a pretty amazing week just hanging out with Ethan. Ethan had gone back to school already, but I had hung out with him after school, when I wasn't out looking for a Homecoming dress, resting, and getting better. It was probably in that order too, but hey, I really needed a dress for the school Homecoming Dance!

That reminded me, I was going to have a ton of homework to catch up on when I did go back to school on Monday. I hadn't done anything besides read novels, watch movies, and recuperate and I knew I was going to be totally behind in my classes. I didn't look forward to that. My usual pile of homework was always enough work for me and only just balanced out okay with my after school job at the Palos Video Store. Focus, Kait, focus. You're about to be at the Homecoming Dance with Ethan Ripley, now is not the time to worry about making up homework or think about going back to work.

Ethan and I were about to walk into the Homecoming dance together. A few weeks ago I never would have believed that this moment could happen even in my wildest dreams. Just goes to show you, anything is possible!

We handed our tickets to the teachers at the front entrance and walked into the main hallway. There were a few couples talking in the hall, but I could see that the majority of them were down the way near the lunchroom and the gym. Ethan and I walked slowly down the corridor. We were about to make our entrance. I felt a little nervous.

"You ready for this?" Ethan asked, grinning down at me.

Ethan thought I was worried about nothing. He just didn't understand because of course, he didn't need to be worried, he was Ethan Ripley and used to the whole being popular thing. The only thing popularity had gotten me, though, was a weird girl reputation, so I was understandably nervous. The whole school was about to watch our entrance. That totally freaked me out.

I nodded despite my nerves. Still, I couldn't help but hold my breath as we walked closer and closer toward the area where the entire school was probably gathered, watching and gossiping about the arrivals of all of the new couples like we were on the red carpet of some Hollywood awards show. I knew we were going to be a huge target for the chatter. I braced myself.

Then we were in the lunchroom. I knew people were staring. I wasn't the expected girl that Ethan would bring to the Homecoming Dance and I knew it, even if he didn't seem to get it. People expected someone like my ex-best friend Ariel to be on Ethan's arm. She was popular and gorgeous and well, at the dance with someone else. A college guy, Troy Matthews, that I met and went out on a date with first and introduced her to, actually, even though she's my ex-best friend. I could see a circle of Ariel's friends and hanger-oners surrounding them at a table just inside the gym, next to the dance floor. Ariel was playing the - I'm here with a college guy card for all it was worth. That was so totally Ariel and one reason we weren't friends anymore. There were a lot of other reasons too, of course.

I knew I was being overly insecure about walking into the dance with Ethan and about what other people might think. I couldn't help it. The thought that the most popular guy at my high school might just actually like me back totally freaked me out. That sort of thing only happened in movies like *Sixteen Candles* or *She's All That*, not in some weird girl who crashes funerals' life. Yet, it was really happening to me. It was flipping me out, albeit

4

in a good way.

"Want to dance?" Ethan asked, breaking into my a zillion miles per minute thoughts. "Yes," I said, gratefully. Anything was better than standing in the lunchroom awkwardly, watching all of the people look back at us and gossip to each other.

Ethan didn't seem to notice, though. I really envied that quality about him - the obliviousness to all the gossips. He just went with it and then did his own thing, no matter what they said. It was pretty cool, actually. I admired him for that.

Ethan took my hand and led me toward the gymnasium. My heart did a little flip as his hand touched mine. I couldn't help but gasp as we walked all the way into the gym. It had been transformed into a romantic Homecoming Dance room. Yes, it was still the gym where I was forced to play basketball and volleyball (and I was horrible at both), but there was something about the decorations and all of the dressed up couples. Sure, the gym was only decorated with cheap streamers, balloons, handmade signs, and paper mache, but it was still breathtaking just because it was very simply, the most romantic moment of my life. At least it was the most romantic night so far.

I gripped Ethan's hand a little tighter. He smiled down at me. I smiled back at him. I wished it could all last forever.

Ethan led me toward the dance floor, past groups of people that I had stopped paying attention to because for me, it was suddenly just Ethan and I at the dance. For at least a moment, nobody else mattered. I didn't even care what song was playing. My first high school dance with a date and we were actually going to dance! He wasn't one of those - I don't dance guys, where you spend the whole night staring at each other and eating way too many of the chips and cheese and crackers because you have nothing better to do. I've been there and done that when I've gone by myself, which I did once.

It was freshman year and I'd gone to the Homecoming Dance alone, mostly to just see what it was like. Well, and my mom really wanted me to. I mean, the way everyone built it up, it was supposed to be this amazing dance, really romantic, and tons of fun, except that it totally wasn't. First off, Ariel, who was still kind of my friend at the time, ditched me for her new friends, Sarah and Megan. Ariel and I were already getting rocky in our friendship, but I didn't expect her to start making fun of me to her new friends when I approached her at the dance. I left after they started laughing at me. Then I spent about ten minutes trying to look absorbed in the food at the snack table. That was, until I noticed that Ariel and her friends were going group to group to say something mean about me. So, I hid in the bathroom for an hour before calling my dad and asking him to pick me up.

Actually, I ran into Ethan on the way out of the bathroom that night, now that I thought about it. He smiled at me in greeting as I walked toward the exit, while he walked back toward the gymnasium. He was being polite and didn't know me, I knew that even then, but the kernel of my crush started growing with that slight encouragement. We'd already met before, when my mom was in the hospital, but he didn't remember that, I didn't think. Maybe somewhere in the recesses of his head, a kernel of a crush had been growing for Ethan too that night. Maybe. Probably not, but Ethan still made my night by smiling at me even if it didn't mean anything. That night, it was the only encouragement I'd had - the one bright spot. I got home and my mom was already way sick with cancer by then and I didn't have the heart to tell her how much that Homecoming Dance totally sucked, so I told her about the boy who smiled at me outside of the bathroom instead. Consequently, my mom thought I had an amazing time because I had developed a crush. I was pretty gushy about that smile. I'd admit to that, but the truth of the matter is, crushing is never fun if it's unrequited. Now, once it's requited...that is a totally different story!

At least I was finally getting that great experience I had heard so much about. I wished I could share it with my mom now, when it was actually true. A wave of sadness blew through me. I missed my mom. I wished she could have known that a mere year later, I'd be at the Homecoming Dance with the smiling boy I had gushed on and on about.

"Kait!" I heard a girl yell behind me and it shook me out of my thoughts.

Ethan and I had just reached the other dancers and were about to join them. I turned to look, wondering if the call was for someone else. I didn't really have any good friends in high school at the moment, but there was always a first. Ethan followed my gaze.

Surprised, I looked to see Suzie Whitsett dragging Kyle Jones towards us. I felt a sudden warmness fill my heart at seeing my friends from Chemistry class. This was the first time I had ever seen them outside of our Chemistry classroom and they were actually acknowledging me instead of pretending they didn't know me. It wasn't me being insecure, by the way, talking like that - it was the simple truth. Ever since my ex-bff Ariel and I had ceased being friends, I had become the freaky weird girl and I had stayed that way all through high school so far. So, this was a very nice first - being at the dance with a date and stopping to talk to what might just be blossoming from more than just lab partner friends into real friendships.

"You guys look so great," Suzie gushed. Normally she was the quiet girl, but since I had helped her and Kyle get together, it didn't seem like she was so quiet around me anymore.

I felt myself turn beet red at the compliment anyway, "Thanks. You guys too."

Suzie turned the full force of her smile on Kyle. He stared back at her like there was no other girl for him in the universe. They were such a ridiculously cute couple.

"Hey, man," Mike Finnigan said, suddenly appearing next to Ethan. He was at the dance with one of Ariel's bffs, Sarah, and had dragged her along to say hi to his best friend. I could tell Sarah wasn't so thrilled to see me, although she was probably taking mental notes so that she could relay them back to Ariel.

I looked around for Dave Rickerson who wasn't usually far behind Mike and Ethan, but he must have been dancing with his date. I wondered who he had brought to the dance. Wow, we were almost starting to form our own group, Ethan and I. It was an odd group too - a strange mismatch of popular kids and totally unpopular kids. Luckily, everyone was being nice to each other despite that, at least so far.

I was only just getting to know Ethan's friends, Mike and Dave, but I liked them a lot. They had come to visit me in the hospital even though they were just Ethan's friends. Their motto seemed to be that any friend of Ethan, was a friend of theirs and they thought it was really cool that I had helped him find out what had really happened to his half sister. Nobody had believed in

Ethan's suspicions at first, that she had been murdered, except me, and Ethan had turned out to be right. The fact that I believed in Ethan and supported him in his search, thus, gave me mad points in Dave and Mike's book.

"You look hot, Kait," Mike said to me, to his date Sarah's annoyance.

Ethan smiled and squeezed my hand. He and I both knew that Mike was just trying to make me feel comfortable in their group. Still, I glanced at Sarah again and hoped she'd complain to Ariel about me. She didn't need to know that Mike was just being nice to me.

"Thanks, Mike," I said, smiling back at him.

There was a bit of a silence as our weird group took each other in. I tried to think of something to say to kick-start the conversation, but I was drawing a blank. Mike and Ethan were both sports nuts although Ethan also wrote songs and avidly read sci-fi novels. Kyle was mostly into all things science. Suzie liked to read about as much as I did, which was a lot. I had absolutely no idea what Sarah was into besides make-up and boys. We were all pretty different, actually.

"So, the gym looks pretty cool," I said lamely to our group, trying to break the awkward silence.

"The Pep Club decorated it," Sarah said proudly, like she was the Pep Club, instead of just a member. "Well, with the help of some other clubs too, but I was here until late last night decorating."

"It looks great!" Suzie said, chiming in.

Everyone took a second look around, as if just taking in the decorations. I mean, it was super romantic, but I just noticed it was themed too.

"I like the theme: A Night in Paris. Super romantic," I said, trying to keep the conversation going.

It was well done, actually. There was a big banner at

the front of the gym, where the DJ was, announcing the theme for the night. A fake Eiffel Tower stood in the middle of the snack table, separating the snacks and the beverages. An Arc De Triumphe was the entranceway into the gym. The tables scattered around the dance floor were covered with white tablecloths and silver stars. The mood lighting was ultra romantic, with small fake candles sitting on the tables.

"Yeah, it was all Madison's idea. She's our club president. Ariel said it was her idea, of course, but I heard Madison suggest it first," Sarah said.

I stopped myself from asking more about what Ariel had said. Was Sarah really criticizing Ariel? Was there dissension among the new group of bffs? I was dying to know, but there was no way Sarah was going to give me any juicy gossip if I asked her. The group lapsed into silence again. What were we going to talk about?

"It looks very cool," Ethan said, trying to get the conversation started again.

The first notes of a romantic slow song were starting to play. I started swaying to the music. Couples formed all around us. We all watched them as we tried awkwardly to think of a conversation piece.

"So, how about we dance?" Mike asked Sarah.

"I'd love to," Sarah said.

"Bye guys," Mike said, as Sarah dragged him away, totally grateful at the chance to get away from us.

Kyle turned to Suzie, "You want to dance too?"

Suzie nodded and turned to us, "See you guys later."

Then they walked away too, hand in hand. Ethan and I were finally alone. We stared at each other, suddenly awkward with one another. I felt a little nervous. We had been about to dance before, but suddenly the air was charged with possibilities.

"Dance?" Ethan asked.

I nodded and took his hand. Ethan led me a little ways onto the dance floor and placed his hands on my hips, drawing me toward him. I hooked my arms around his neck. I caught the scent of his cologne. He smelled amazing. We started moving to the notes together, side to side. My stomach was doing nervous excited flips. Now this was the best moment of my life.

Ethan looked down at me and I looked up at him, our eyes meeting. I leaned up to kiss him. I really couldn't have asked for a more romantic Homecoming Dance moment. It was so perfect, but just as our lips were about to touch, we both jumped as the music stopped with a screech, ending in dead silence. Then I heard the girl screaming, and screaming, and screaming.

CHAPTER 2
GAWKING

Within about five minutes, they cleared everyone out of the school. I had never seen the staff and the students evacuate the building so fast. I think they did it even faster than during a fire drill, actually. It was pretty impressive.

The police arrived within fifteen minutes and I saw Detective Dixon among them. I recognized him right away from the Styrofoam cup he was carrying in his hand, which he promptly threw into the trash on his way into the building. I needed to send that guy an anonymous letter about recycling and the environment. Or, maybe I should just drop off a travel mug for him at the station. Anonymously.

Everyone was gossiping and rumors were rampant. The latest thread was that Casey Hunt had found a girl dead in the girl's bathroom. Casey was a junior and a popular girl wannabe, so some people were questioning if her story was even true or if it was an elaborate popularity stunt. In my head, I thought it could go either way. I wasn't a huge fan of Casey's, being that she, like Ariel, enjoyed making fun of me as long as it made her look cool. Still, the police being involved definitely made it look legitimate. I couldn't see Casey lying about finding a dead body and calling the police if it wasn't true.

Supposedly, Casey had been about to go in and pee, when she opened the bathroom stall, which was unlocked, and found a girl dead in the stall. According to the rumors, there was blood everywhere, like in *Kill Bill* style, but somehow I thought the gossip mill was starting to embellish the gore. We weren't in a slasher movie like *Friday the 13th* or something. Someone would have heard the murder happen if it wasn't quick. So, the exact cause of death was unknown and probably greatly exaggerated by all of the student gawkers.

The thing was, nobody seemed to know who the dead girl was and if she was a date from another school or if she was someone we all knew. People were checking on their friends, to make sure they were okay. It was really kind of scary. I glanced around for the people I'd be worried about, like Kyle and Suzie from Chemistry class. And, of course there was Ariel, but I had to remember not to care too much about her. Still, I saw that she was okay and happily clinging to her date, Troy.

That's when I noticed that Troy was looking at me. I managed a smile. I liked Troy and if I hadn't been totally gaga over Ethan and been wrapped up in a murder mystery where Troy was the prime suspect when I first met him, well, we might have had a shot. Troy smiled back at me and waved. That's when Ariel noticed that he wasn't paying attention to her and started in on him. His attention quickly focused back on her. Poor Troy. What had I gotten him into by introducing him to Ariel?

I was happy to have Ethan by my side, holding my hand in his. He was actually pretty quiet now that I thought about it. I looked at him in concern. I totally understood if this was bringing back bad memories for him. I mean, we had only just solved his half sister Liz's murder and here there was another murder, mere weeks after her death. I wouldn't blame him for freaking out a little. At least her murderer was behind bars, awaiting trial, and would hopefully be put away for a long, long time.

"You okay?" I asked, squeezing his hand.

Ethan looked at me, like he just realized I was there. "Uh, yeah. Sorry. I was just thinking about Liz."

I nodded. I knew it. Ethan frowned at me.

"What?" I asked.

Ethan seemed to think better of what he was thinking, "Nothing."

"You sure?" I asked. Ethan really looked like he wanted to say something, but was torn about saying it. It felt like it might be important. I waited, watching him look at me indecisively.

"Well," Ethan started and then hesitated again. "I was just going to ask you not to get involved in all of this."

"All of what?" I was confused.

"The murder investigation," Ethan said simply.

This time, I frowned. "What makes you think that I would do something like that?"

Ethan smirked at me, "Do I need to remind you how impulsive you were when you stole off with Troy by yourself to get information out of him? Or, when you taunted Liz's killer and almost got yourself killed?"

Ethan did have a point. When I got it into my head that I was right, I didn't pay any attention at all to any realistic opinions even if they were coming from my crush object. I never realized I was so impulsive, though. I guess I really could be when I thought I was right. The thing was, I had done the right thing in all of those instances - those impulsive moments had helped us move forward and solve the case.

The funny thing about this whole conversation, though, was that I hadn't even thought about investigating this murder. Ethan had asked me to investigate Liz's murder with him. It hadn't been my idea. Well, okay, maybe I had offered to help him out of the goodness of my heart and my huge crush, but Ethan was the one who had started investigating first! So far, I hadn't even considered looking into this murder. I didn't think I had, at least. I mean, I was as curious as the rest of the student body about what had happened. It did just shock and freak out everyone at the Homecoming Dance, which I had been attending. For all I knew, it could have been me. That was scary. The poor girl. Her poor parents. They all deserved to know who killed her.

Okay, maybe Ethan had a point because now I suddenly did want to investigate the case. The way he was looking at me, though, sent off warning bells in my head. Even though I had successfully helped him solve his half sister's murder, Ethan didn't want me near this one.

"I promise," I heard myself whisper as I stared into his eyes.

Ethan smiled back at me and I saw the tension around his eyes, dissipate, "Thank you."

That's when I heard it. The girl in front of me whispered it to her date, but I suddenly heard a collective whisper as the gossip passed from group to group, "The dead girl is Madison Brown. She's a senior."

I felt a chill crawl up my spine and goosebumps form on my arms. Did I know her? The name sounded really familiar. I couldn't wait to go home and look up her yearbook picture to find out who she was or her profile, if it was public. It really could have been any of us. I wanted to find out who did it. Uh-oh. Suddenly I realized that it was going to be really, really hard to keep my promise to Ethan, maybe even impossible.

CHAPTER 3
GRAVEYARD CRASHING

I went to visit my mom at the graveyard most Sundays. In the spring, I planted flowers. I wasn't a gardener by any means, so I planted whatever was decently priced and pretty and hoped it would all look nice in front of the headstone. Mostly, I hoped they would make it through at least one season. I knew my mom wouldn't care anyway about what kind of flowers I'd planted. She'd just have appreciated my effort. Then, in the summer, I tried to keep the plants alive in the muggy and super hot heat. The fall had me trying to help them survive for as long as it stayed warm enough and when it finally turned toward winter, I brought cut flowers when I could and just laid them in front of the headstone.

When it was nice outside, I actually brought my lawn chair and a book and just spent the day with my mom at the cemetery. Is that weird? Maybe it was a little different to most people, but it was not totally unusual, actually. Culturally, people did it. Okay, maybe they didn't do it in American culture, but other cultures did have more rituals and customs concerning the dead and their spirits and the afterlife. Consider the Latin American holiday Dia de Los Muertos or in English, The Day of the Dead, where the celebrants build elaborate alters to the deceased and celebrate with their favorite foods and beverages. The intent is to encourage the spirits of the dead to visit their living loved ones. I think that sounds pretty nice, having my mom come and visit me. Still, I wanted to visit her more than once a year. I'd take what I could get on her part and just hoped her spirit stopped in when I was there.

Today, I planned on just sitting with my mom for the day at the cemetery. It was always quiet and serene there. It was probably a good place to meditate actually, if you were into that kind of thing. I needed to think. Originally, I planned to share the details of my date with my mom and the romance of the Homecoming Dance to make up for the lie about the one I went to when she was alive, but the murder at school the night before had shaken me up. I had even dreamt about it. I was a detective trying to solve the case, but just as I was about to uncover the real killer, I woke up. Figured. I hoped Ethan wouldn't be mad at me for dreaming about solving the case. I knew there was a part of me that wanted to do it in real life too, but I had promised.

I hadn't even gone home to look for Madison Brown in my school yearbook, like I wanted to. I stayed off of Facebook and her wall and didn't look at my Twitter stream to see what my fellow classmates had been posting about the dance and the murder. I had changed into my pajamas, taken the pins out of my hair, washed the make-up off my face so I wouldn't get a zit, and went to bed, cuddling with my cat, Scarlett. So, I had been good so far about keeping my promise to Ethan. Well, except for the dream where I had been a detective.

I set up my lawn chair, sat down, and turned on my brand new e- reader. My dad thought I'd love it and gave it to me when I was in the hospital. He was right. I was super excited about getting it. In fact, I was so excited, I didn't know what to download first. I mean, I loved my book, books and I'd always have a bookshelf of the real deal. The cool thing about the e-reader, though, was that it let me carry around a gabillion books at once. I could have my whole bookshelf with me at all times. It was almost as great as Wired's peanut butter banana milkshake. Almost. I had downloaded four books so far. Not that many for a week spent relaxing, but Ethan had distracted me for part of that too, well, him and getting ready for the Homecoming Dance.

I perused my books. I was going to read Amanda Hocking's book *Switched* first. It was inspiring that she had become an indie bestseller and besides, I loved paranormal romance. So, if it was anything like *Twilight* or *The Vampire Diaries*, I was in. I was just about to start on the first chapter when I saw one of my graveyard friends. No, not one of the walking dead - zombies aren't real.

It was this little old lady who came to visit her husband's grave. Her name was Leonora Viola and she had to be in her late eighties, although I had never actually asked her specifically. She and her husband, Jacob, had this great love affair. They met as kids in the 1930s or something like that and he was the only boy she ever dated. They got married after high school and they lived happily ever after...until he died. She had never felt heartbreak until that day and it almost destroyed her. He was the love of her life and since now he was dead, she made it a point to visit him and keep him as a part of her life. It was the only way she could deal with it. Leonora complained about her kids, who tried to urge her to move on. She didn't want to move on or meet someone else. She was eighty plus years old. She didn't want to wash another man's socks and cook him dinner. She was done with that. Jacob had been the love of her life and there wasn't going to be another one like him. She had no urge to settle. Leonora wanted to spend her free time reading, knitting, and watching old movies, especially ones that she and Jacob had watched during their lifetime together. The rest of her time Leonora wanted to spend at the graveyard, chatting with her husband.

I know a lot of people would think that was totally weird and that Leonora should see a psychiatrist, but I thought it was sweet. Besides, she was eighty something and she didn't seem depressed or anything otherwise. Leonora knew she had a great life. She always talked about how lucky she was that she had met the love of her life so young, married him, and had a wonderful life with him. She still wanted him in her life, even if it was just chatting with him at the graveyard. Like me and my mom, this was the closest Leonora and I were going to get to a relationship with the people we had loved and lost.

So, despite the age difference, we had become great friends. We understood each other. While Leonora wanted to chat and spend time with her husband, I wanted to spend it with my mom. Most of the people in my high school didn't get that. I didn't blame them. Funerals, graveyards, and the like are creepy when you have your whole life ahead of you and don't even think you could possibly ever die. Most of the kids my age had never really known anyone that had died. Even if someone like their grandparents did, they considered them a billion years old and it didn't quite reach them that it was real and a part of life. I knew about real death, though, because of what happened to my mom. So did

Leonora. Her kids misunderstood her too, just like the people in my high school. We weren't morbid, wanting to spend a day or two a week in the graveyard. We were visiting the people we loved.

"Morning, Kait," Leonora said, walking over to me after she said hello to her husband.

"Morning, Leonora," I said, putting down my e-reader.

"I read the story in the paper about the high school. Did you go to the dance? Are you okay?" Leonora asked.

She didn't know anything about the whole Ethan's half sister's murder mystery and that I had been shot. I hadn't been to the cemetery in weeks, actually. I had been too wrapped up in crushing on Ethan and solving the murder mystery. If Leonora had known about that, I knew she'd freak out. She liked me a lot, sort of like a granddaughter, really. It was sweet and I felt the same way about her. She was like my grandma and I didn't want to give her a heart attack or something by telling her. So, I just answered her question, without going into details about the real things I was thinking about - like Ethan, solving the murder, and my promise.

"I'm fine," I said. "And, I was at the dance."

Leonora grinned, ignoring the whole murder aspect of the Homecoming Dance immediately, "With a boy? Is it like I said with my Jacob? Did you feel that spark I told you about? Like the one I felt that day Jacob walked me home and I just knew?"

I tried not to smile too big. Leonora had known Jacob was the one since he walked her home from school one day when they were kids. Well, teenagers. It was hard to think of Leonora as my age, but she must have been about the same age when Jacob walked her home, give or take a year, and she fell head over heels in love with him that day.

Things were different now. Nobody walked girls home from school anymore. Well, basically nobody walked. And, Ethan and I had just started going out. I mean, I didn't know if we were technically even dating. How did you know? I mean, we had gone to the dance together and he had kissed me a few times before that. Was that dating? And, then if we were dating were we boyfriend and girlfriend? I mean, I thought you'd just know, but I didn't. It wasn't like we had decided on it or anything. It was all so confusing. Was it supposed to be as easy as just knowing like Leonora said? Was it bad that I didn't already know? Were we doomed? Now, I was suddenly worried. Wait, I didn't need to be worried. Ethan like liked me. I think.

I ignored my inner turmoil, not wanting to bother Leonora with my mental battle about the status of my and Ethan's relationship, so I smiled and said, "Um, I don't know. I mean, I like like him, but we just went to the dance together, so..."

"Maybe bring him by sometime?" Leonora asked hopefully.

I nodded before I thought better of it. Sure, Ethan knew I crashed funerals, but he didn't know I hung out in the graveyard and had graveyard friends. Did I want to introduce him to that world too? I wasn't so sure. He had been so accepting of the funeral crashing. That was one thing. Hanging out in graveyards was another. Still, I couldn't disappoint Leonora. All of my grandparents were dead. She was the closest thing I had to a grandma. It seemed kind of fun thinking about her meeting Ethan, eventually. Like, after we decided if we were really going out. I was a little afraid she'd interrogate him, actually, now that I thought about it.

"So, are you going to that girl's funeral?" Leonora

asked.

"Who?" I asked and then remembered after I said it. My brain had been on Ethan, which sometimes glitched my brain into forgetting everything else. Leonora knew about my hobby crashing funerals.

"The girl from the high school who died," Leonora reminded me. "So sad. She was so young. Too young. In this day and age, I can hardly believe it when I read a story like that. You be careful, though. Sounds like some nutcase is on the loose."

I hadn't thought much about it. I mean, even if I wasn't investigating, should I go to Madison Brown's funeral? My brain had been focused mostly on Ethan and the dance in the last week and now, it was mostly on Ethan and the mound of homework from school that I was going to have. Well, and ignoring the fact that I wanted to investigate the murder. Normally, I'd have already found the girl's obituary and started doing research on her for the funeral. Since she went to my high school that would have been easy enough. I just had to pull out my yearbook and check Facebook and Twitter. Madison was bound to be somewhere in one of those online mediums.

"Maybe," I said, wondering if Ethan and I might make plans instead. "Depends on what else is going on."

Leonora looked at me knowingly, "Sounds like love to me."

I felt my cheeks turn pink. I wished I could hide my emotions better. This was embarrassing. I hoped Ethan couldn't read me like that yet. I wanted to be cool, sexy, and mysterious to him.

Leonora frowned, "Just make sure he treats you right. A gentleman should always open your door. And, don't let him kiss you right away. And, make sure you keep him on his toes. Make him work for your affections. And, don't always do what he wants you to - be your own woman."

"Okay," I said, almost choking on my saliva at the last piece of advice.

Leonora did have a lot of life experience and she was pretty much telling me to go with my gut on what I did with my life. Currently my gut really did want to solve this murder mystery. Was this life's way of telling me to go for it, despite my promise to Ethan?

I decided to clarify, to be sure, "So, Leonora, are you saying that you didn't always do what Jacob wanted you to do?"

Leonora looked at me incredulously, "Goodness no. If I did, we would never have done anything exciting. He was a homebody, always happy to stay at home and read the paper when he wasn't at work. I was the adventurous one and booked vacations for us and forced him to get out and see the world."

"Didn't he get mad at you, though? Like when he wanted to just stay home?" I asked.

I wasn't quite sure that investigating a murder was like getting your husband out of his lazy comfort zone and off the couch and into the world, but I was curious now about what Leonora would say. She did have a lot more life experience on the subject than I did.

Leonora sighed, "Sometimes. But that's the thing about love. He always forgave me, no matter what."

I nodded, pondering. That was a true enough statement, I thought. If Ethan really like liked me, he'd see that I had to investigate and find out what happened to Madison. I had even dreamt about it. I wanted to help, just like I had wanted to help Ethan find out what happened to his half-sister. It hadn't been all about my crush that time either. I genuinely wanted to make things as right as they could be in this messed up world, by giving the grieving left behind some kind of closure. He'll love me no matter what, I told myself. Or, well, at least like like me, since I didn't exactly know where we stood just yet on the whole love thing or even the dating thing. How did you find that out anyway?

CHAPTER 4
SECRET SLEUTHING

Feeling immensely lighter at deciding to break my promise to Ethan, for his own good, and to keep us out of a comfortable box, I went straight home from the graveyard, dug out my yearbook and looked up Madison Brown. Even from her photo, it was hard to believe she was dead. She had this contagious smile and lopsided grin, like she was always smiling. She had short brown curly hair that looked like maybe it was permed, but it could have been natural with the help of some hair products. She was a senior this school year, so I didn't really know her and she wasn't in any of my classes, but besides recognizing her name from the night before, I found that she did look familiar for some reason. I stared at her picture, but nothing came to me. I looked at the list of activities under her name, wondering if that might give me a clue. Maybe she was a cheerleader or something, she kind of looked cheer-y.

Then I saw it. Madison was in a club: Pep Club. The group that had helped decorate the dance last night according to Sarah. I looked at Madison's picture again. It totally fit with that grin of hers, actually, but that's where

I knew her. I had idiotically tried to join Pep Club at the beginning of the school year and it had been a total disaster. My dad had drilled it into my head that I needed to start thinking realistically about colleges. My grades were decent. They were nothing like the straight A's Ethan got or anything. Still, I mostly got A's and B's and I was pretty happy and proud of that. Although, I would have done cartwheels if I ever got straight A's. There was always just one class, though, and usually at least two that always prevented that from happening.

Anyway, I thought Pep Club would be something easy to do, as far as clubs went. I mean, you just went to games and made signs and stuff. It was all about school spirit. I could do that without too much effort. And, I didn't mind the effort of a club or anything. There were just no clubs that I really wanted to join. Still, my dad said I had to join something and so, I decided on Pep Club.

I knew the cheerleaders, the jocks, and most of the popular kids went to all the games from football to basketball to whatever, but people like Ethan went to all the games too. And, I had already thought he was cute. So, what was wrong with spending a night here or there watching some cute guys play sports and cheering them on? Especially if one of those guys was Ethan?

It sounded like a good idea at the time, but when I got to the first Pep Club meeting, I found Ariel there. Sarah and Megan were probably there too, but I focused on Ariel. I mean, didn't she have boys to chase or something? How did she have time for Pep Club and shopping too? Still, for her, I guess it was an easy club. She was already cheer-y.

So, long story short, the day I signed up for Pep Club, I quit. My name was still on the list, though, and I never actually quit, quit. I just never made it to the meetings. I still planned on putting it on my college applications. I did go to the first meeting, after all. I had the rest of the year to attend another one too, to make it really official. Two meetings was enough, right?

Still, that day proved to be important in terms of my investigation. I remembered Madison pretty well. She was the President of Pep Club. She was super into it too and tried to get all of us potential new people excited and peppy about joining. I've never seen someone so on, unless they were onstage, but this girl was totally all over the place and trying to ramp us up. It would have been a really fun and energetic club meeting too, if Ariel hadn't spent it giving me dirty looks at crashing her club meeting. At one point, I got frustrated enough that I wanted to walk over and tell Ariel off. I didn't know that she was going to be there and the looks were getting super annoying. Not that I was actually going to talk to Ariel and tell her that. I'd let Ariel think that I was trying to follow her or emulate her or something. That was a better revenge. Besides, Ariel would think it anyway. She was narcissistic like that.

I was sure I had seen Madison in school too, but it was definitely that day in Pep Club that I remembered her from. She had been so full of life. Why would anybody want to kill her? And, why at the Homecoming Dance? There were way more private places to kill someone. Was it a crime of passion instead of a planned and thought out crime? That was something to really consider. It would be way better to go after someone in a dark alley than a crowded dance and it wasn't like girls weren't in and out of the bathroom every few seconds fixing their hair and make-up. I was surprised nobody had seen anything.

It occurred to me that school on Monday was going to be insane. Madison Brown's murder was going to be the talk of the entire student body. There hadn't been a tragedy like that in my school since I had been there, so it was going to be interesting to see the after effects. I wondered if they were going to close off the bathroom near the gym that they had found her in. I knew I wasn't going to be paying it visits anytime soon. I'd have to find out which stall too and definitely avoid it. I wondered if prom would be cancelled even though it was seven months away. Would Ethan have asked me? I ignored the thought, instead just hoping that Ethan wouldn't still be mad at me by then for breaking my promise to him regarding investigating the murder. It was important that the case be solved, although a prom date when it came time would be nice too.

I wondered how Madison's friends and family were doing. I felt really bad for them. I knew how big of a hole a loss like that could be, especially when it came so unexpectedly and totally blew your world apart. I opened a window on the internet and logged onto Facebook. I hadn't been friends with Madison, but her profile was public so I was able to check it out without a problem. Her wall was filled with posts from grieving friends. I read through them one by one. Madison sounded like an amazing girl. She seemed like the real deal - smart, nice, peppy, and she had tons of friends. I almost wished I had decided to stay in Pep Club and gotten to know her. Then I reminded myself that doing so would have meant a lot of quality time with Ariel making posters and going to games and I knew it would never have happened.

From Madison's Facebook page I garnered a few tidbits about her: She was a big fan of Lady Gaga. She kept posting lyrics from her songs as her status updates. Her favorite movie was *The Notebook* because it made her cry. On an opposite note, she was a huge sports fan. It looked like she even took part in a fantasy football league, which was so not in type with how she looked. Still, guys probably thought it was super hot. And, Madison loved, loved, loved the Pep Club. There were tons of pictures of her at games, making posters, and cheering her heart out. She was all about the school spirit.

I also noted that I knew some of Madison's friends. I didn't know if they were close friends because it was Facebook and Madison might have just added people and well, I didn't know, know them exactly. Like, we weren't friends, but they were in some of my classes and in my grade, so I knew of them even if we never really talked. I wondered if I should start by talking to them, to get more of an idea about her and who might have had reason to kill her. Then it occurred to me that I might weird them out by doing that. I had never spoken to them before this and the first thing I did when I finally talked to them, was talk about a murder. Yeah, they might legitimately think it was weird.

I opened a window outside of Facebook and googled Madison Brown's name to see if there had been an obituary posted. It was already online, including the date, time, and location of the wake and funeral. That had happened fast.

Madison Brown, 18, died Saturday. She was an honor student at Palos High School. Her motto in life was to live life to its fullest. She always did and will be sorely missed. She is survived by her parents Jennifer and Kevin Brown and her sister, Lana Brown. The wake will be held on Friday from 3-9 pm at Palos Funeral Home. The funeral is Saturday at 10 am.

It was so sad, but at the same time I was surprised. I thought maybe they'd keep the body a little longer to do forensics stuff. Then again, we were in a small Illinois suburb. They probably didn't have a forensics unit.

Maybe I watched too much *CSI*. Actually, I almost felt sorry for Detective Dixon. He was probably buried in paperwork after this sudden jump in the city's murder rate in the last couple of months.

Still, Madison wasn't being buried until late in the week. The police must be holding the body for forensic evidence or something. Usually, people got the funeral over with quicker than that for the simple fact, that you had to get it over with, in order to start moving on with your grief.

Actually, I didn't feel the full extent of my grief over my mom until after her funeral. It hit me a couple of days after and I couldn't get out of bed. At that point, my dad wanted to take me to the doctor and get me on antidepressants, so I dragged myself out of bed and went to school. I'm not a big fan of pills and in my opinion I kind of had a reason to be sad, you know? I was pretty okay after that. Especially after I started funeral crashing and visiting my mom at the graveyard. She kind of found a way back into my life again. What had destroyed me so much after the funeral was that I had thought I lost her entirely, but she was still out there even if it wasn't in exactly the same way.

I found myself thinking back to the dance. If it was a murder of passion, did Madison have a fight with her killer at the dance? Was it someone Madison knew and was friends with? Maybe it was even one of the people posting a sympathy comment on her Facebook wall? Or was it an enemy, someone that hated her for some reason? I looked back on Madison's Facebook page. She was listed as single. I wondered if she had any exes to worry about or a new potential guy that could have turned killer. I knew how that is he or isn't he my boyfriend thing went, so it was also possible that she wasn't single at all. I mean, I was still listed as single on Facebook, technically, and what were Ethan and I? I hoped I wasn't sabotaging myself on that front.

I ignored my thoughts of Ethan and pulled a blank notebook out of my desk drawer. I always kept a couple in case I needed one for school to replace the one I had filled up. I was an excessive note taker. It probably wasn't a good thing. I wanted to write everything the teacher said down, which meant I also had a lot to study when it came time to prepare for a test.

I started writing down the names of Madison's friends. There were over three hundred of them on Facebook. That was a lot of suspects. I stopped. What was I doing? Nobody had asked me to investigate Madison Brown's death and here I was starting to write up a list of potential killers to start crossing suspects off. What was wrong with me? I had almost gotten myself killed investigating the murder of Ethan's half sister. Ethan was totally right. I should stay out of this.

I felt torn. I wanted to investigate the murder and find out what happened. I knew I didn't get to really talk to Madison that day in Pep Club, but she seemed really cool. She definitely didn't deserve to be murdered. I wanted to find out who did it and who took her life away like that. Maybe she would have become the first female president or something equally as cool and society changing amazing, but now it was never going to happen.

I thought about my mom. If I could have prevented her death I would have done it in a heartbeat, but cancer was her killer. Madison's parents didn't even have that knowledge. She was just killed by some unnamed person in her high school girl's bathroom during a dance. It wasn't right. Madison deserved justice. And, besides, what if the killer didn't stop with Madison? What if he or she killed someone else? I couldn't let that happen knowing that maybe my investigation could have stopped it from happening.

I ignored the little voice in my brain that was telling me that I had almost died the last time I had been involved in a murder investigation. The other part of my brain was telling me that there was no way Detective Dixon was going to solve this case without my help. Hey, it had been true the last time.

I continued with my list of potential killers, throwing out names that didn't seem plausible at all. There were twenty-three names in all that I thought were possibilities from their comments on Madison's wall. They were all guesses, in the thought that Madison was killed by someone she knew, in the heat of the moment. Where did I start? The killer might not even be on my list. I didn't know Madison well enough to know if there were other people that could have found a motive. I didn't even know anyone on the inside, who knew Madison well, that I could easily talk to.

An idea I didn't like occurred to me. I scanned through the Facebook posts on Madison's wall again. Ariel had quite a few posts on her wall and not just since Madison died. Madison wasn't one of Ariel's best friends like Sarah or Megan because I saw Ariel with those girls all the time, but Madison definitely seemed like a friend of sorts to Ariel, if the following wall banter counted for anything:

Ariel: Can't wait to mall it up!

Madison: Pizza!

Ariel: Salad! You want to fit in the dress right?

Madison: Only if I can have pizza.

Ariel: Fine. No pepperoni. And we blot the cheese with a napkin.

Sounded like they went Homecoming dress shopping together. That's a big deal for a girl, especially one as into looks, clothes, and popularity as Ariel. So, it looked like Ariel and Madison had grown decently close since the start of the school year. They even had some Pep Club pictures together, making posters. I hated to admit it, but Ariel actually looked happy in the photos and like she was having fun. Maybe I just hadn't seen that side of Ariel in a long time. At this point in our relationship when we were together, Ariel usually scowled at me or made fun of me. Neither was pleasant.

I thought for a moment. Ariel would definitely be the easiest person for me to talk to about Madison, in that I probably could get her to talk to me, if I tried. She did owe me one for roundaboutly introducing her to Troy. I looked through some of the other people who looked to be friends with Madison. Even with going to the dance with Ethan, I was doubtful that they'd open up and talk to me about their friend. I was still the weird girl even if I was dating one of the most popular guys in school. We were technically dating right? I stopped my brain right there and went back to my original train of thought. Yeah, they'd probably think I was obsessing about their friend because she died or something creepy and weird like that and then they probably wouldn't talk to me about anything significant. It could ruin my investigation entirely if people didn't talk to me at all and the graveyard girl rumors spread like fire again.

Yeah, Ariel was the lead I'd have to take. Surely, my ex-best friend would take a moment out of her day to talk to me if...if I made her. The question was, would I be able to survive the conversation?

CHAPTER 5
RECONNECTING

I suppose I should have called. At the time just showing up at Ariel's house on a Sunday in the late afternoon seemed like a better idea. Ariel wouldn't be able to say no to talking to me (followed by hanging up on me or calling me names and then hanging up on me) and that was right, but what I didn't consider was Ariel's mom answering the front door.

"Kait? Kait Lenox?" Mrs. Walker said in surprise.

Mrs. Walker looked the same. I nodded, feeling suddenly nervous. I hadn't considered Ariel's parents. I hadn't seen them in eons and there had never been an official goodbye to them, even though for a period of time, both sets of parents were like my own since Ariel and I spent so much of our time together. What did Mrs. Walker even think of the whole situation? She had to take Ariel's side. Ariel was her daughter.

So, I was a little shocked when Mrs. Walker's surprise quickly turned to excitement. She was happy to see me. That was actually sort of nice. I found that I was glad to see her too. It really had been too long. Too bad I wasn't sure that Ariel was going to be having the same aw-this-is-a-nice-visit reaction.

"How are you? What have you been up to? How are your classes? Have you thought about colleges?" Mrs. Walker asked in a breathless rush, like she knew I'd have to leave once Ariel came into the picture and she wanted to get all the questions out in time before then, "I haven't seen you in such a long time. Are you here to see Ariel?"

"Yes, actually," I started, thinking rapidly. "I just needed to get some notes from her. I spilled pop all over mine and I know she has the same class."

Mrs. Walker considered this, "You know, you should stay awhile. You girls haven't hung out in ages and you were such good friends. I'll make a pizza."

I froze. I didn't want to disappoint Mrs. Walker, but I doubted Ariel was going to want me to stay the thirty minutes it took to make a pizza. Ariel probably wouldn't want me to stay the length of time it took to make a bag of microwave popcorn, which on my microwave was three minutes. I had it down to a science.

"Ariel!" Mrs. Walker called before I could think of a way to dissuade her from making the pizza, "Ariel! There's a friend here to see you!"

"What, Mom?" Ariel screamed from her room up the stairs.

I heard Ariel's bedroom door open and then listened to her heavy barefoot footfalls as she walked to the top of the stairs. I had a clear view of Ariel as she froze there, in shock at seeing me in her house. We stared at each other.

"It's Kait, Kait Lenox!" Mrs. Walker said, as if she had to clarify this to Ariel, who I've gone to school with and known since forever, "Isn't it nice that she came over?"

Ariel declined to reply and instead walked down the stairs slowly, as if she was trying to give herself time to figure out what in the world I might be doing at her house. By the time she made it to the bottom of the stairs, Ariel had a deep frown on her face. She was definitely thinking something.

Ariel put on a fake smile for her mom, "Yeah, it's great. We're going to go talk in my room, Mom. Okay?"

"Great! I'll make that pizza," Mrs. Walker said, running off to the kitchen before Ariel could try and dissuade her. She seemed so happy. Both of us just looked after her helplessly.

"Ariel," I said, as soon as her mom seemed out of earshot.

"Let's talk upstairs," Ariel said and motioned me to follow her to her bedroom. "My mom will totally eavesdrop if we talk down here."

As much as I hated to admit it, I knew Ariel was right. Her mom was so excited that I was over at their house that she'd be dying to find out what we were talking about. She probably had this misplaced idea that maybe I was there to make up with Ariel. I was sorry to disappoint her. If that was ever going to happen, Ariel would have to make up with me. And, just to use the cliché saying because in this case it was probably true - it would be a cold day in hell if that ever happened.

Besides, if Ariel was going to flip out on me and throw me out, I'd rather her do it out of earshot of Mrs. Walker. I was kind of glad Mrs. Walker still liked me, even if Ariel didn't. They really had been a second family to me for a long time when we were friends. Then when I lost Ariel's friendship, I lost them too.

I was in Ariel's bedroom for the first time in just over two years. It was amazing how much it had changed. When we were friends, her walls had been decorated with pictures of us and ripped out pictures of celebrities from our favorite movies and television shows. Now, all of the posters were gone. Her room had become more adult with white bare walls with red trim and a pop art looking painting of a sky of hearts on one of the blank walls of the room. The only traces of the old Ariel I knew were on her makeup table and her mess of a closet - full of trendy up-to-date clothes. She had always been all about being a girly girl and loved fashion and makeup. I should have seen the popular girl high school train coming from a long ways away, but I had thought our friendship could survive anything. It had survived junior high intact, after all. Still, I was wrong. High school was a whole different animal.

Ariel shut the door and turned to me, seriously, as soon as the lock had clicked into place, "I'm dating Troy. You have Ethan. End of story."

It took me a second to follow her train of thought. Ariel thought I wanted to talk about Troy and dating him again. The one and only time I had dated Troy, I had been helping clear him as a murder suspect in Ethan's half sister's murder. The date, unbeknownst to Troy and Ariel, had been a ruse to get information out of him. Troy was pretty cute and maybe if I wasn't dating Ethan, I'd go out with him again, but I would never in a million years try and steal a guy away from a girl. Even if that girl was Ariel. It just wasn't my style. I believed in true love and I wasn't going to be the reason someone else broke up.

"This isn't about Troy," I said, simply.

"It's not?" Ariel looked confused. "Then what do you want?"

"I wanted to ask you about Madison Brown," I said.

"What? Why?" Ariel looked suspicious. "Are you trying to get into her funeral or something?"

"No," I shook my head, "It's not about funeral crashing. You seemed like you were her friend and I just wanted to know a little bit about her."

"Are you going to her funeral?" Ariel asked flatly.

I was honest, "Probably. I genuinely want to know about her, though. I'm not trying to exploit her. I mean, does that really seem like something I'd do? You know me, Ariel, even if we aren't friends. I know you remember all the sleepovers we had and the best friend bracelets and stuff, you know who I am. I genuinely want to know about Madison. I swear."

"But why?" Ariel asked again. "There has to be some kind of angle. I mean, you showed up at my house and talked to my mom. That's crazy."

"I know," I said. I thought fast. Should I be honest with Ariel? Or not? I felt weary about it. The last time I had been honest, Ariel had told the whole school about how I crashed funerals. From then on, I was a graveyard girl. Not a good nickname for a high school girl if you ever wanted to have a social life, even a small one.

The funeral crashing started about a month after my mom's funeral. I was still really struggling and I happened to catch the obituary section of my dad's newspaper. Yes, he still got the real paper. He was old school and liked the idea of the real thing. I started reading them and found myself fascinated that so many people died. I mean, it made sense, but I never really thought about it until it happened to my mom. People died all the time, of course, but until then it hadn't happened to someone I knew. Then I saw there was a wake being held that night, just after I got out of school. So, I decided to go. The people there would know how I felt. I wouldn't be alone.

It was the best decision I ever made. The deceased name was Jacob Viola. That's right. That's how I met Leonora. Her husband's funeral was the first one I crashed, although we didn't talk too much that night. I was sort of out of it when I went. It immediately brought back memories of my mom. Some people started talking to me and I had no idea about any of the rules to not getting caught funeral crashing and said I was a relative when someone asked how I knew the deceased. They assumed I was a granddaughter and brought me over to say hi to grandma. Except, Leonora didn't know me. That's when Ariel swooped in and saved me, even though she didn't know that's what she was doing. I had made a fateful mistake. It turned out Leonora was Ariel's great aunt and Jacob was her great uncle.

Ariel claimed me as her friend and then took me off to the outside back of the funeral home to talk. At first, Ariel, very typically, thought it was all about her. She thought I had stalked her to her great uncle's funeral. That was so not true. I wouldn't have come if I'd known Ariel would be there. We weren't friends anymore and she made fun of me every chance she got. Still, I, in a moment of weakness, admitted that I was funeral crashing. I tried to explain how alone I felt and why, but Ariel must not have heard me continue on after my grimly shocking revelation. Thus, Ariel found out the one thing that I would have definitely kept a secret if I had taken the time to think about it and hadn't been in a really vulnerable state of mind.

I trusted Ariel and of course, she took the opportunity to blab it to the rest of the universe known as our high school. I guess it would have been a totally awful night if I didn't run into Leonora as I was trying to get out of there, away from Ariel and her freaking out about my weirdness and wondering how we had ever been friends. Leonora had stepped outside for a breath of fresh air. I was crying and she stopped to ask me what was wrong and then we connected despite the vast age difference.

Leonora started telling me about Jacob and I started telling her about my mom and it was like kismet. It's the one thing I really love about funerals, the sharing of stories and the remembering of loved ones who were gone. It created a bond between Leonora and I, although I made sure she never told Ariel about it. Leonora, at least, could keep a secret.

I hesitated a little longer as I thought about if I could tell Ariel the truth about investigating Madison's murder. I knew Ariel and deep down a part of her still had to be the same girl with whom I had grown up. When we were kids, Ariel and I really were the best of friends. I had one memory when Ariel had this favorite toy. We were about five. It was this doll that Ariel always carried around. For some reason, I took a fancy to it and asked her if I could borrow the doll. Her name was Miranda. Ariel freaked out and burst into tears, but after her mom calmed her down, Ariel let me borrow the doll because I was her best friend. It was only for a day, but still. Her mom didn't force her. She wanted to lend it to me to be nice because I was her friend. That had to still be there, somewhere inside of Ariel.

I took a deep breath and then just said it. Maybe it was foolish, but a part of me hoped that Ariel had grown as a person in the last year and wouldn't just announce my plans to the whole school so that she had some ammunition with which to make fun of me, "I'm investigating Madison's death. I want to find out who murdered her."

"What?" Ariel looked at me in shock. "Are you crazy? You almost died like a week ago and now you want to go chasing after some murderer again?"

I was shocked into silence. She and Ethan had the same reaction to my investigating this murder. That was weird, right? They should in no way be on the same wavelength. Ever.

"Yeah," I said finally.

"Why?" Ariel asked, frowning at me.

I thought about this for a moment. "I just feel like her parents and the people who loved her deserve some answers. They should know who did this to her and why, so they can be caught, charged with murder, and go to jail. If my mom's cancer could have been locked away in prison, I'd feel much better, but all I can do about that is donate to Ovarian Cancer Research and try to do Cancer walks. I'm totally for both of those and I do think they really help the cause, but at least with Madison, I can personally dig around and see if I can find anything out. Maybe I can help her family and friends deal with what happened."

Ariel looked at me like I was insane, "But that's the police's job."

"Yeah, I know," I nodded. "And, they're great at it, but if I happen to find something out, it's not going to hurt. And, I'll tell them all about it. I swear. I'm not dying to get shot again or anything."

"Wow," Ariel said, "I never thought I'd say this, but you should just stick to funeral crashing."

I shrugged. Ariel was probably right, but I couldn't help myself. I wanted to find out what happened to Madison and who was it going to hurt if I did a little asking around about her friends and enemies? If I didn't find anything out, nobody would even know and if I did find something, I'd go straight to the police. I, in no way wanted to put myself in danger again. I had learned more about hospitals in the last week than I cared to know.

Ariel sighed, "But you're not going to, are you? I just don't get you, Kait. You can be so totally smart, but sometimes you just throw it away on the wrong things."

That's where Ariel didn't understand me and it was the crux of why we had stopped being friends. Our values were different. She coveted the acceptance and admiration of her peers. For her, the wrong things were anything that didn't make you popular. As much fun as popularity looked, I didn't actually need it. So, those things that Ariel thought were important, didn't mean anything to me. Sure, it made life a lot easier if people thought you were awesome, but I shouldn't have to be someone I wasn't for that to happen. I was just me and that was all I wanted to be.

"I am who I am," I said.

Ariel looked at me and seemed about to say something, but changed her mind as she exasperatedly said, "Fine. You want to know about Madison? I'll tell you all I know about her. Where should I start?"

Mrs. Walker chose that time to knock on the door. Ariel and I froze as if we were doing something wrong by being in her room together, talking like almost friends.

"Pizza's ready!" Mrs. Walker yelled through the door.

It had only taken Mrs. Walker about fifteen minutes to make the pizza. She must have known my time was limited. Mrs. Walker was using her time wisely to keep me there a little longer by forcing me to eat.

Ariel unlocked the door and Mrs. Walker brought in the pizza. I didn't realize how hungry I was until I smelled the freshly baked dough and cheese. Yum. Ariel didn't look as thrilled. She was probably on a diet. I remembered her wall banter with Madison about eating salad and not pizza. I took a big bite of my slice and looked at Ariel curiously, as she blotted away at hers with a napkin, getting off all the grease.

"So, you were friends with Madison?" I asked again,

after Ariel had relocked her bedroom door and we were sure Mrs. Walker was out of earshot.

"Yeah," Ariel said, taking a tentative bite of her pizza, "We were both in Pep Club together. That's how I met her, actually. She was a senior and I mean, I saw her around school because she was always involved in stuff, but we had never talked until the beginning of this year when I joined Pep Club."

"What was she really like?" I asked and took a big bite out of my slice of pizza. It was good. I wondered what brand Mrs. Walker bought. We needed some more good pizza to eat in the freezer at home.

"She was amazing," Ariel gushed, thinking about her friend, "I mean, Sarah and Megan are my bffs, but Madison was really starting to be a good friend. I mean, we just went shopping for Homecoming dresses together and I don't just go to the mall with anyone."

I knew that was a dig at me, but I ignored it. In the weeks before our friendship had blown up, Ariel blew me off to go shopping at the mall with other friends - namely, her new, more popular, cooler friends, Sarah and Megan.

"Can you be more specific?" I asked. "Like what were some of her key character traits?"

"She was really positive and upbeat although she could be a little sarcastic like you sometimes. It was just in a funny way. She was a lot of fun to be around," Ariel said. "Like when we were dress shopping, she said the funniest thing and..."

Ariel froze. I could see that it had just occurred to her that Madison wasn't going to be making any more funny comments, ever. Ariel's eyes started tearing up. I didn't know what to do. I would have hugged my old best friend, but since we weren't friends, I wasn't sure how to react.

I moved toward her, but Ariel stepped back in reaction and wiped at her eyes quickly. I tried not to feel hurt as I saw the mask come down over Ariel's face, hiding her emotions from me. She was always trying to maintain the cool. It finally occurred to me how really hard that must be for Ariel to do, especially when she was hurting.

"What about her close friends? Who were they?" I asked, trying to ignore what had just happened. I knew Ariel would prefer it. Besides, I had an idea about this from the posts on Madison's Facebook page, but it would give me more evidence if Ariel actually told me who her friends were.

"Leslie Frank, Dana Julian, and Desiree Reed were her closest friends, I'd guess," Ariel said.

I nodded, " They were in Pep Club too, right?"

"Yeah," Ariel said, "Why didn't you stay in Pep Club anyway?"

Ariel remembered that I was there. Why did she care if I quit anyway? I mean, I couldn't exactly tell Ariel that seeing her there had made it a total turn-off for me to ever go to another one of the meetings again, especially since Ariel was being so nice to me at this very moment. I didn't want to piss Ariel off just as she was opening up to me.

I shrugged, "I just got caught up with school and work and stuff. No time."

"Funeral crashing?" Ariel said haughtily.

So much for Ariel being nice. Still, I ignored her, "So, did Madison ever fight with her friends or anything?"

"You think they might have killed her? That's laughable. You are so not good at this detective thing," Ariel said. "They're so upbeat and awesome. No way."

"Well, I have to ask and not assume," I said flatly, refusing to take Ariel's bait to start a fight.

"Well, if you asked me who might have had a good reason to murder Madison, I'd tell you to check out Noah Robertson," Ariel said pointedly. "Noah definitely had a reason to off Madison."

I didn't know Noah Robertson, although I vaguely thought he was a football player. I'd have to look him up in my yearbook and online to get a clearer picture of him.

"And what was that reason?" I asked.

Ariel paused for effect, "Well, Madison was all excited after the first football game and she was jumping around, doing cartwheels and stuff. We were all goofing around. Noah wasn't paying attention and she accidentally tripped him. It was a total accident, but Noah broke his leg and he's a senior, so that means he won't get to play his last season when it might be important for college scouts to see him. He was super upset about it and harasses her all the time now. Well, harassed. I'd say Noah Robertson should be your number one suspect."

CHAPTER 6
HEAD SPINNING

My head was spinning by the time I got home. For one thing, I had just spent over an hour talking and hanging out with Ariel and we hadn't killed each other. Sure, there had been moments where we almost went for each other's throats, but all in all, it was almost kind of, sort of, dare I even think it...fun? I mean, besides the very somber topic of death and murder. Still, things had gone so well, it had to be an anomaly. Ariel and I didn't hang out...anymore.

More importantly, I hadn't thought about Ethan in at least three hours. Oh, and I had my first murder suspect. Of course, I wouldn't have a chance to try and purposely run into Noah Robertson until tomorrow morning at school.

I also needed to track down Casey Hunt and hear her account of finding the body. That was where Detective Dixon had a leg up on me. He had a legitimate reason to ask people about a murder case. I didn't. Still, I was hoping Casey might talk to me. I was hoping she'd talk to everyone, actually, just to keep the gossip train focused on her. She did like the attention, normally. That would make it easier for me to approach her anyway, if she was being super open about it. Casey might have seen something that could help me pinpoint the killer. I could only hope.

Going back to school after having been out of school for a week was always a shock. Everything changed and yet it was like you had never left. Even though I didn't really have any friends, I still missed out on any of the little dramas that made school interesting. Okay, maybe I did listen to some of the gossip. It was definitely more captivating than some of the lectures. It was like a real life soap opera going on around me, you know? And, speaking of getting behind, need I mention, all the homework? The teachers were all sad and sympathetic that I had been in the hospital, but not enough to let me out of doing the assignments entirely. In fact, I had to make-up everything. It was so unfair. Did they know how much work that was going to be?

Everyone was a little distracted, though, at school. The high school had used the murder as an incentive for better security since it was obvious that the "it will never happen at our school" attitude wasn't true. Metal detectors were being installed at all of the entrances and a couple of off duty policemen were stationed at points around the school. It was definitely about time for us to catch up with the times. It's sad it took a tragedy to make the school revamp their school safety protocols.

Besides that, the murder of Madison Brown was by far the hot topic of the school and to my dismay, Casey Hunt was nowhere to be found. The rumor was that she was hiding out at home. It was totally out of character for her, but Casey had found a dead body, so maybe she was still in shock or having a nervous breakdown. I could understand that. The gossip vultures were definitely going to pounce once Casey came back to school and she should be ready for it. It was disappointing, though, Casey's account of what happened was pretty important to my case. I'd have to hope, for now, that she came back to school in the next couple of days. Otherwise, I might have to hunt her down since I didn't see Detective Dixon giving me a copy of Casey's police statement so that I could read it.

I kept a lookout for Noah Robertson, who would have no reason to skip school, unless he was on his way to Mexico, but I didn't see him in the first two hours. I wasn't even sure what I was going to say or do when I saw him. I mean, I couldn't exactly go up to him and say, "Hey, did you murder Madison Brown? Oh, and can you tell me your motive?"

It was before third period and I was rushing to my locker to grab a book, so I almost missed him. It was obviously Noah, though. He was tall, broad shouldered, and had brown hair clipped super short, like he had let a buzz cut grow out. I don't know what was wrong with me because I didn't even stop to think about it as I walked as hard as I could into him. It's not like little old me was going to make a dent in this massive guy, but then again Madison Brown had managed to break his foot by accident. Still, at least I took the time to notice that Noah was wearing a walking cast on his right foot and smashed into him on the other side.

As I felt myself fall backwards, my books scattering out of my arms, I pondered the intelligence of my choice. Sure, it had worked with getting to meet Troy. And, really, I couldn't just walk up to a random guy in high school and start talking to him out of the blue, could I? That would be crazy. So, yeah, the old fallback, run into someone and run into them hard, had to work.

"I'm so sorry," I said automatically as my butt hit the hard tile floor. I did mean it. I shouldn't have run into him so hard. That hurt.

Noah was still standing, looking down at me with a frown, like I was a total idiot, and didn't saying anything to me. Then he just turned and walked away, leaving me looking stupid, sitting on the ground with my books scattered down the hall. I could hear a couple passersby snickering because they had seen the impact, my fall, and the odd results. I ignored them and gathered up my books. Okay, obviously the old run into him as hard as you can fallback didn't work. Now, I had a lead in to talk to Noah, though. I definitely wouldn't mind yelling at him for ignoring me when I apologized to him. That was totally rude. Did the guy have no manners? I glanced around, suddenly anxious. Okay, good, Ariel hadn't been witness to this. That, at least was promising. I ran to my locker, grabbed my book, and made it to my third period class just as the bell rang.

I kept a watchful eye out for Noah as I walked to my fourth period Chemistry class, but we didn't cross paths again. I was still mad even though an hour had passed. My butt still really hurt. I was almost positive that I had a black and blue mark from my fall. I didn't see why Noah couldn't even acknowledge me when he was the person that had made me hit the ground. Sure, I had made it happen, but Noah didn't know that. He was so totally rude. Maybe it was just this easy and I had stumbled across the killer right off the bat. Either that or Noah sure had a lot to learn about manners. I really couldn't wait to find him again so that I could tell him off and, of course, continue with my murder investigation.

I made it to class a couple of minutes before the bell and saw Kyle and Suzie talking at my lab table. I felt a pang. Even though Madison Brown had been murdered, it looked like Kyle and Suzie's big Homecoming date had been a huge success. Suzie's hand was on Kyle's arm and she was laughing. Kyle was smiling up at her from his chair like she was the only person in the entire world. I, on the other hand, didn't know where I stood with Ethan and I had repeatedly broken my promise to him in the last twenty-four hours. That probably didn't bode well for any romantic thoughts I was having.

I hesitated in the doorway, not wanting to interrupt Kyle and Suzie's moment, but I didn't have anywhere else to go, so I moved forward and toward them. Besides, my books were heavy. I had to put them down before my arms fell off. My butt already hurt. I didn't want to add my arms to the list.

"Hey guys," I said cheerily as I walked behind Kyle to sit in my lab chair, setting my books down on the table in front of me.

Kyle and Suzie both looked over at me, surprised. They had been so absorbed in their world that they hadn't even paid attention to me walking around them. Wow, was I like that with Ethan? I hoped so.

"So, how'd your date with Ethan go?" Suzie asked, entwining her hand in Kyle's.

Yeah, they were totally an official couple if they were holding hands in public. I wondered if they had defined themselves. Were they officially boyfriend and girlfriend now? I felt a little more envious. I really wished I knew what was going on with Ethan and I.

I shrugged, "Good, well, except for the whole cancelling of the dance because of a murder thing."

Kyle nodded, "I know! I was so glad Suzie was with me at the time. She had just gone to the bathroom like fifteen minutes before they found the body. She was so lucky nothing happened to her."

Suzie smiled at Kyle, "You would have protected me, though, right?"

Oh dear, they were going to be one of those super cutesy couples that drove you insane to be around with all their cute talk. Then again, I would have given anything to do the cutesy thing with Ethan, so I was a total hypocrite. Was breaking my promise going to affect us doing that? I pushed the worry away and focused. This was important too.

"Did either of you guys know her? Madison?" I asked. Even if they weren't bffs with Madison, any details other than what I knew could be helpful just because they were from another angle.

Kyle shook his head. Suzie paused. I looked at her curiously.

"I kind of knew her," Suzie admitted after a moment.

If I was the suspicious type, I'd be finding it very numerically insane the amount of people that Suzie came into contact with that got murdered. And, she was a quiet girl who kept to herself and did nothing wrong, so it was a weird coincidence. I mean, what were the odds, you know? She didn't know that many people. Still, it wasn't like Suzie was the rebellious type who went out of her way to find trouble. Or, was there more to Suzie than I knew from seeing her every day in Chemistry class?

"How'd you know her?" I asked after Suzie didn't say anything more.

"Well, I used to know her. She and I had this tennis camp together the summer after sixth grade. Madison was a year older than me and in seventh, but at tennis camp it didn't matter," Suzie said. "I was terrible at tennis and hated it, but my mom forced me to finish camp anyway. Madison hated tennis camp too, so we bonded and spent the afternoons after a morning of getting yelled at for being terrible tennis players, getting ice cream, going to the mall, or catching a movie. We both gained like five pounds that summer with all the junk we ate. She joked that we were going to have peanut butter M&M, cinnamon bun, popcorn, soda babies with all the junk food we were eating. It was a really good summer and we kind of stayed friends when school started up, but it wasn't the same. Because Madison was a year ahead of me, we never had any classes together and Madison had her own school friends in her grade, so we drifted apart in the first couple of months after the school year started. Then one day Madison just stopped calling me back. I didn't talk to her for a while after that, although I probably saw her from a distance here and there at school, but we never spoke. Then I ran into her at the beginning of the summer before I was going to be in eighth grade, so before her freshman year, and she was totally different from the Madison I was friends with in tennis camp."

"Peppier?" I offered.

"No," Suzie said, "Totally depressed, actually. I mean, we complained about tennis camp, but we had a lot of fun and a lot of laughs anyway. The Madison I ran into that summer was almost totally out of it and a little chunky, like she had totally let herself go."

"What? But..." I started trying to wrap my head around the idea of a depressed Madison. It was impossible. All I could see was the peppy girl I had seen at the first Pep Club meeting - the girl who was full of life and positive energy.

Suzie shrugged, "I don't know why she was depressed or anything. I mean, maybe when I saw her she had just broken up with a guy or something. But still, you could tell she had major problems and I only talked to her for a few minutes."

I was still trying to grasp a depressed Madison and I had to say it, "But she was president of the Pep Club."

"Well, only this year. She must have gotten better over the last two years. Or gotten meds or talked to a counselor or something," Suzie started, thought for a moment, and then continued, "And, that happened by her junior year because I saw her at a bunch of basketball games cheering like a maniac with the Pep Club last year and she looked totally alive again and way healthier."

"Can you think of anyone who might want to murder her?" I asked.

Suzie looked at me strangely, "Are you investigating again?"

"You did just get out of the hospital," Kyle warned me. He was always so realistic and rational. That's probably why he was a science genius. Still, did everyone have to take Ethan's side on this? I had a side too.

Suzie and Kyle were in the small group of people who knew the whole story about how I had ended up in the hospital. At least, I think they were one of a few. I didn't seem to be the talk of the school so far. Then again, there had been a girl murdered at the Homecoming Dance over the weekend, so that might have blown any story about me being a female sleuth in addition to a funeral crashing graveyard girl weirdo out of the water.

"I was just curious," I said, not wanting to admit my sleuthing to anyone in case Ethan found out by way of casual gossip, "So, can you think of anyone?"

Suzie gave me a look, but instead of questioning me on my motives again she thought for a moment and said, "Maybe."

"Who?" I asked after Suzie didn't say anything more.

"Well, if I had to guess a suspect, and I mean, she may not be guilty at all..." Suzie started.

"Just say it," I demanded. Suzie was the type to feel guilty about naming names and normally I would too, but this was murder we were talking about.

Suzie sighed and then said, "Madison's ex-best friend, Julia Morgan. They were friends forever, even when we were in tennis camp, but at the beginning of this year, they had a huge falling out when she claimed Madison stole the Pep Club presidency from her."

"How do you know about that?" I asked, wondering why Ariel hadn't said anything about Julia. Then again, maybe Ariel was friends with Julia too and biased against her being a murder suspect. "You're not in Pep Club, are you?"

Suzie shook her head adamantly, "No. It's so not my thing to yell and cheer at games. I'd rather be reading a book. Actually, I kind of know this guy Logan who used to be friends with them too in junior high and he's the one that told me that Julia and Madison had a huge falling out about Pep Club."

I had no problem believing the idea that the killer was a girl. Girls could be just as murderous as guys when they put their minds to it. Was the Pep Club presidency worth a murder sentence, though? I didn't know Julia Morgan. Still, it was possible that she thought it was completely worth it. I mean, crazy was crazy. I'd have to talk to Julia and see what I could find out.

"Do you think Julia really could have done it then?" I asked Suzie to clarify.

Suzie shrugged, "Who knows, you know? I didn't know her that well even when Madison and I were friends, just because a big group of us only hung out a couple of times. Still, the one thing I do remember about

Julia, though, is that she was kind of ruthless. Madison got this shirt for her birthday that Julia wanted, but her mom wouldn't pay for it, and Julia spilled fruit punch all over Madison on purpose, to ruin it when we were at the mall. Things like that."

I nodded, considering this. Spilling punch on your best friend's shirt wasn't the same as murder, but I still put Julia on my short list to talk to, right behind Noah. For Madison being such a happy peppy girl, I was surprised how easily murder suspects were finding their way out of the woodwork. Of course, I was only at two real leads, but I wondered how many more would be on the shortlist by the end of the day. It was only fourth period and I hadn't even really done much investigating yet.

The bell rang and Suzie kissed Kyle quickly on the lips and ran to her lab table. They sure were disgustingly cute and I probably would have teased Kyle about it as we prepared for our Chemistry lab, but I was too busy thinking about what Suzie said. I had my second suspect. I was going to have to think of a more clever way to talk to Julia Morgan. The bump into a person had lost its effectiveness and I didn't have much hope for the just talk to them tactic either. I guess I could lie and come up with a clever facade, a part to play that would get people to tell me what I wanted. That worked in books and movies too. The problem, as far as high school went, was my weird girl reputation. People already assumed I was a certain type of person and I couldn't break that stereotype in one conversation. I'd have to ponder further.

My stomach grumbled. I was already hungry for lunch. I didn't want to be. Lunch meant seeing Ethan and I'll admit it, I was a little nervous about that. Did I admit to breaking the promise? Or did I just not say anything so that by the time Ethan found out, I'd already have solved the case? Maybe Ethan would be really proud of me instead of mad? I hoped.

CHAPTER 7
LUNCH SLEUTHING

I walked into the lunchroom and looked over toward my usual spot. Ethan had joined me for lunch a few times before my hospital stay and it had definitely made us the gossip of the school. Then we had gone to the dance and sealed our high school reputation as a dating couple. At least that was my interpretation of things. The question was, would Ethan take this time to get some space from me and sit with his friends at lunch or would he further cement us as a couple to the student body by officially sitting with me at lunch again? It was a good question and that and the breaking of my promise were both warring with my thoughts as I walked toward my lunch table.

I was disappointed to see that Ethan wasn't at my usual table as I walked by it to the cafeteria food lunch line. I glanced over to see if he was with his friends at the popular table, but he wasn't over there either. I hurried into the lunch line and ordered cheese fries and a Coke. Murder investigations made me want junk food. Maybe Detective Dixon had something similar going on with his Styrofoam cups.

Besides, I deserved the grease, caffeine, and sugar after

the hospital stay and everything. I actually missed the high school cheese fries, even if that was crazy. I hurried through the lunch line and paid the cashier with exact change. I didn't want Ethan to not see me at my usual table and think that I was the one that needed space or something.

Rushing toward my lunch spot, just in case Ethan decided to show up and hadn't because I wasn't there, I felt my heart plummet a little. I really wanted to sit with Ethan at lunch today. I wanted to spend the hour hearing about his classes or the latest sci-fi book he was reading or the song he was working on. The last time I saw him, he had dropped me off after the dance, after the police had cleared us away from the murder scene. It was definitely an anticlimactic end to what was supposed the have been the most romantic evening of my high school life. Ethan hadn't even kissed me goodnight. We had both been distracted.

And, we hadn't talked since then. Of course, it had just been a short twenty-four plus hours, okay more like thirty something hours. I felt a pang in my heart at the thought of more time passing without talking to him, especially if Ethan was only across the lunchroom sitting with his friends. That was a no man's land to me. Unless Ethan invited me, there was no way I was going over there to sit with him.

Wow, was I really this obsessed with Ethan? I couldn't help wondering if this was what it was like to fall in love. Or, maybe it was just me going crazy because they sure felt pretty similar and I was very confused.

I walked toward my lunch table feeling more melancholy. Ethan wasn't there. He wasn't having lunch with me. Oh well, I forced myself to think, that's okay. No big deal. I have a murder mystery to solve and suspects to think about. I had my crime notebook and my cheese fries and my caffeine filled, sugary soda. If I really got bored, I could do my makeup homework. I'd totally be fine.

That was when I slammed full force into Noah Robertson again. My fries went airborne. The lunch tray slammed into my chest, spilling cheese and fry grease down my shirt. This was not good. I didn't have a change of clothes and it meant that I'd have a stained shirt for the rest of the school day. Just what I needed to remind people what a freak and obvious klutz I am.

This time it was a total and complete accident on my part. I didn't even see Noah. I definitely would not have purposely spilled cheese all over myself. This was high school. I didn't need the mortification.

"Did you do that on purpose?" Noah was glaring at me.

With some relief, I noticed that I hadn't smashed into Noah anywhere near his hurt foot. It would totally have been an accident if I had. Seriously.

I felt my anger from our morning meeting returning. And, yes, that time I had purposely run into Noah, but this time really was an accident. Didn't this guy know the simple words I'm sorry? Geesh.

"No. What the hell is wrong with you?" I felt my anger rising, along with my voice. I was mad and I rarely got mad, "I should be asking you the same thing Mr. I Can't Apologize Because I'm Way Too Cool For That Since I Play Football. I have cheese all over my shirt. Do you know how embarrassing that is? I have to wear this shirt the whole rest of the school day. I would not have done that on purpose. And, how rude can you get? No, I'm sorry or anything? I mean, are you a total dumb jock or what? I hate to apply stereotypes here, but come on.

Really? All you had to do was say I'm sorry, but noooo..."

I was on a roll. I was venting. This felt good. Why didn't I do this more often? I should express myself like this all the time, especially to Ariel. It didn't even cross my brain to actually worry that this guy was a buff football player, potential murderer, and could use my tirade as a motive to kill me. At least until this very second, when I stopped short at that thought.

"Whoa," Noah said, backing away from me and holding up his hands. "Calm down. Sorry, okay? Sorry."

His apology completely deflated my sails, that and the fact that he might kill me for going off on him if he was the murderer. Besides, the apology was all I had really wanted even if he was only probably saying it because I was flipping out on him. I didn't hold my anger long usually anyway, "Okay. Thanks."

Now it was awkward. Noah was staring at me and I was staring at him. There was silence.

"Fine then. I'm going to my table," Noah said.

"Wait," I said. He totally did not mean that apology and both of us knew it, but I held my tongue. "You owe me."

"I owe you?" Noah looked at me. "For what? Crashing in to me twice today?"

"No. For this," I said pointing at my shirt "This cheese is not gonna be coming out anytime soon and I like this shirt. A lot."

It was true. I had picked out my shirt purposely as my back to school after being gone a whole week shirt. Plus, I had wanted to look cute for Ethan. Now I had cheese all over me. Maybe it was good that Ethan was sitting with his friends today. I didn't need him to see me like this.

Noah frowned, definitely wanting to get away from

me, but probably not sure if I'd run after him and cause another scene. He looked torn. I needed to convince him.

"I just want to talk to you for five minutes," I said simply, trying to sound as rational and normal as I could, "Five minutes and then you can go."

Noah studied me with narrowed eyes for a moment and then said, "Fine."

I led Noah back to my lunch table. Ethan still hadn't showed up, I found myself thinking. I pushed the thought aside by reminding myself I was covered in cheese and probably did not look my best. I had to focus. What did I ask Noah? Did I just ask him about Madison up front? Hint? What was the best approach? Actually, the decision was easy. I was lucky if Noah would even give me five minutes to talk.

"How did you know Madison Brown?" I asked, seizing the day, and just going for it.

Noah almost dropped the soda he was about to sip, despite the fact that Madison's name was probably one of the most popular topics in school. If Noah had spilled his soda all over me too, I found myself thinking, I would have killed him on the spot and then we'd be talking about another murder. Overreaction? Yeah, probably, but I didn't need to add to the lunch mess on my shirt. It would really ruin my day.

Noah was sputtering, oddly terrified that I was asking him about Madison, "What? Why? Do you think I did it or something? That's insane. A guy can't go into a girl's bathroom. There were like teachers around watching out for that stuff."

It was so weird. One minute Noah was calm and the next he had totally flipped out and snapped into this strange freaked out mental state. That was something to note.

"Uh," I was surprised that Noah was flipping out. I didn't know what to say. My brain couldn't grasp onto any ideas about how to calm him down.

"You should talk to Sebastian Zane, that's who you should talk to. He freaking took Madison to the dance. He was totally messing around with her. He's probably the one that did it. Why the hell are you talking to me?" Noah was the one on a rant now.

It was kind of scary seeing it from the other side, I had to admit. Still, we were in a public place. It wasn't like Noah could attack me in the middle of the lunchroom, right? I got ready to bolt anyway, just in case he gave me a reason to run.   Until then, this was a fascinating development.

I also made a mental note to check out Madison's date to the dance. That should have been an obvious one to put on my list. I just wanted to talk to Casey Hunt first, find out if she had seen anything when she found Madison. I guess the whole girl's bathroom thing, had me wanting to lean toward a female killer. I had to remind myself that a murderer might not care what it said on the door. Regardless, Noah, was rapidly becoming number one on my list with this potential toward a freak out by me just asking him a couple of questions about the murdered girl.

"Calm down," I said slowly and calmly, "I'm just talking to you."

"Well, I'm not talking about Madison! I don't care if you got cheese on your shirt!" Noah yelled and got up, stalking away from me.

Whoa. Now Noah was the one causing the scene and I was definitely the center of attention at lunch again if all of the eyes staring at me were any measurement to go by. That's when I saw him - Ethan. He must have gotten to lunch late because he was just walking out of the lunch line. Normally, Ethan ate pretty healthily or brought a lunch from home, but today he was carrying one of those pre-packaged cherry pies that I had told him I was craving in the hospital. I knew that tasty treat was meant for me. Ethan was the sweetest, most romantic guy ever. I felt my heart melt.

Then I noticed the expression on Ethan's face. I registered hurt, then anger, and suddenly Ethan wasn't moving toward my table anymore.

CHAPTER 8
HEART BREAKING

I spent the first part of lunch gazing over toward Ethan's table as he talked to Mike and Dave and some of the other people at his table. Some of them were girls. I felt a pang of jealousy. Ethan had his back to me the whole time and didn't even look at me. He was totally mad and yet, I couldn't bring myself to walk the distance to his table and apologize for breaking my promise. I had known in my heart of hearts that Ethan was going to be angry about it all, but somehow I had convinced myself that it would be okay in the end. Now, I wasn't so sure that things were going to be okay. We had been on the maybe boyfriend/girlfriend track, but it was now looking like we might be on the maybe broken up track.

I couldn't even eat my cheese fries, I was so upset about the tension emanating across the lunchroom between Ethan and I. I knew he had to be talking about me to his friends too because I saw Mike try and sneak a glance at me. Then when I caught Mike's eye, he looked guiltily away. Dave was more stoic, but I'm sure he was dying to look too.

I knew I should just suck up my pride and walk over

there and tell Ethan how I felt and how much he mattered to me and that I was sorry, but I just couldn't do it. Part of it was that all of the people sitting at Ethan's table intimidated me in some way. They were all popular and by default I felt inferior at the power they held at this school. Still, if that was all, I would have done it - gone and apologized. What was stopping me was that Ethan mattered to me so much that I just didn't know what to say. An apology didn't feel like nearly enough. What if he didn't hear me? What if he stalked off? Or worse, what if he yelled at me?

Ethan and I had gotten into disagreements before, of course. They mostly had to do with his half sister's murder case and at the time, our differences in opinion were on investigative styles and suspects. This was different, though. Back then, we had just been tentative friends and I didn't expect Ethan to stick around and actually be my friend for the long haul. When Ethan asked me to the Homecoming Dance, though, and spent those couple of days with me in the hospital, all of that changed. Ethan became a part of my life. I wanted him there for a good long while too, maybe even forever. The problem was, now it looked like I had ruined everything.

There was a question bothering me. Was it worth it? Who was right? Was I wrong to investigate the murder? Was he wrong to ask me not to? Sadly, I didn't think it mattered because I just kept coming back to the fact that I had, regardless of right or wrong on the issue, broken a promise to someone I cared about, someone who trusted that my promise was real. I had betrayed Ethan.

I knew I needed to stop staring at Ethan's table longingly, but I couldn't focus on anything else. I thought about jotting the latest in my crime notebook, but now case solving left me with a sick feeling. I had let Ethan down.

I still needed to go and clean off my shirt. It was pretty gross. I took one last long look at Ethan's table and went to ask a teacher for permission to use the bathroom.

After a few minutes of rubbing a wet paper towel on my shirt, the stain didn't want to completely come out. I gave up and dabbed at it a few more times. My shirt was now soaking wet. The day could only get better, right?

"You okay?" a girl asked from the doorway.

I looked over and watched the girl walk into the bathroom. I hoped she hadn't been there for too long watching me fight the stain on my shirt. It was not my best moment. Wait, should I be nervous that there was a stranger in the deserted bathroom with me? I thought of Madison and wondered if I was being silly, feeling suddenly on high alert.

I didn't know the girl. She had long blonde hair with dark brown and red highlights, so her hair looked sort of multicolored. I knew she wasn't in any of my classes, so I had no idea why she was suddenly next to me, peering at my face, looking concerned.

"Who are you?" I had to ask. I blurted it out too, but I hoped I didn't sound too rude. I just didn't have the energy to be polite and she was kind of creeping me out.

"Julia. Julia Morgan," Julia smiled and I saw that she still had braces.

I wasn't sure what to say. Julia had sought me out instead of the other way around. I hadn't even had a chance to find a picture of her yet so that I knew what she looked like and here she was standing in front of me. That was kind of weird. Cool, but weird.

It must have sucked to have braces as a senior. Most people had them off by sophomore year. I wondered if the braces had been what hurt her chances for the position of Pep Club president. It didn't matter to me, but the sad fact of it was that it was a high school reality. People were that judgmental about things like that. Braces really could have meant the difference between her and Madison for president.

"Uh, why are you here?" I asked awkwardly. I didn't know how else to ask it or what else I might say to be less blunt and besides, as Anne Shirley from *Anne of Green Gables* would say - I was in the depths of despair about Ethan and I would have preferred to be left alone to wallow if I had the option, that and to continue getting the stain out of my shirt.

"I heard that you're looking into Madison's murder," Julia said. "Is it true?"

I felt my stomach sink. People knew. Wait. How did they know? Although Noah's outburst had been a great hint at that, most people other than Ethan wouldn't actually assume I was investigating Madison's murder. Even me talking to Noah about the murder, regardless of the fact that he had gotten so upset, wasn't that out of the ordinary. Everyone was talking about the murder. Ethan definitely would not have publicized the fact that I was playing teen sleuth, except maybe to Dave and Mike in the form of complaints, and only in the last five minutes when he figured out what I was doing. I groaned inwardly. This was Ariel's doing. Ariel had gone and gossiped about my investigative plans to who knows who. Now, the school was going to think I was a funeral crashing, witchcraft practicing, drug dealing, pet cemetery caretaking graveyard girl female sleuth. And, no, ninety-nine percent of that sentence was not true, but according to the rumors I seemed to have quite the amazing reputation for being a girl that in reality, mostly just went to classes, work, and every once in awhile, funerals.

So much for thinking that maybe Ariel and I had bonded the night before. Although, I would admit, I didn't exactly tell Ariel not to tell anyone that I was looking into Madison's death. I had hoped she wouldn't, but I hadn't actually said anything to her about it. I didn't really want to give her any ideas, you know? Still, you'd think she'd have some common sense that I didn't much like being the butt of her gossip and might pass on some gossip of my own, like that we had hung out at her house and had pizza.

I had to admit, though, that in this case it seemed like Ariel had actually helped me. Julia might not have talked to me on her own and I definitely saw what a disaster talking to Noah out of the blue had been. So, I took a shot and was honest.

"Yeah, I'm looking into it," I said.

"Have you found anything out?" Julia asked.

I wondered if Ariel was paying me compliments because Julia actually sounded like she thought I might be doing a good job as an amateur detective, "Still in the beginning stages. You were Madsion's best friend right?"

Julia hesitated, "Used to be one of them. I mean, I wish we had made things up before she died, but it wasn't meant to be."

"What happened?" I asked, even though I already knew. I just wanted to see how Julia would interpret it.

"Well, she became the biggest bitch," Julia said simply and then rushed on as if she had been holding the whole thing in for too long, "She stole the Pep Club presidency from me. We've been best friends since we were eleven and she gets the opportunity to be president of a club we're both in and she totally backstabs me. I told her I wanted to do it, be the president. Then, she put her name in the hat too."

"So, you guys just broke off a friendship because you both wanted to be Pep Club president?" I asked.

There was definitely more to my and Ariel's friendship ripping apart than some stupid club presidency. This was high school, though, and that sort of thing could really, really matter here. And, okay, maybe mine and Ariel's breakup had to do with the popularity issue, which was also way high school or maybe it was just time that we parted ways. Maybe it was the same for Madison and Julia too.

"No," Julia shook her head, "It was the way Madison treated it. Like suddenly she was so much better than I was. I knew Madison could be like that, all hoity-toity and stuff, but she had never turned that on me. Suddenly, Madison started acting like I was the dirt underneath her shoes or something. I mean, I knew all her dirty little secrets, we were friends since we were kids after all, and believe me, no matter what I've done, hers weren't pretty either, but Madison badmouthed me to all my friends in the club anyway."

"What did she say?" I asked.

Julia smirked, "Oh, she was good. Madison told the girls in the club that I was secretly after their boyfriends and that if they weren't careful, their guy would be hooking up with me after school. Madison claimed I had done it to her. And, if she was talking about Logan, it was in junior high, and we went out for a day. Big deal. It was junior high. I didn't even know they were dating. That's lame and it was so a billion years ago. We were just kids. Or, even Ray Newton. I mean, he dates someone new every week. Besides, you'd think some of these girls would talk to each other and find out that Madison was telling them all the same thing. I couldn't be after everyone's guy, you know? It's statistically impossible. But no, they were all freaking out and jealous and wondering if their guy was cheating on them. It was insane."

"What did she tell the guys? I mean, Pep Club does have guys in it right? The girls couldn't just push you out," I said, and besides I was curious. Julia was making me think that Madison was a lot like Ariel, spreading stories and that was a totally different picture than the one I previously had of Madison.

"There are way more girls, actually, but Madison didn't have to tell the guys anything. Once she turned the girls against me, the guys were already turned. Ninety percent of them are only in the club to meet girls anyway. They're not jocks, so they have to talk to them somehow. They weren't going to go after the girl who was alienating all of the other girls and risk making their dating pool into a pool of one," Julia charged ahead, venting her frustrations.

"Wow," I said.

That was really mean of Madison. I had no idea from what others had said so far that she had such a cruel streak in her. Madison wasn't just a peppy, sweet, nice girl that was unjustly murdered. There were some ugly layers underneath. Maybe there was a good reason for it. Maybe it was the call of the Pep Club presidency that had caused her to act that way. Still, she had pretty much stepped all over a friend and made pretty permanent dents in said friend's high school social life. Was that a good enough reason for murder?

"Yeah, it totally sucks, right?" Julia said. "I just couldn't believe Madison shattered my reputation like that. I couldn't even get a date to the Homecoming Dance. I had to go with a friend. And, I totally had to drop out of Pep Club even though I loved it. It was just too miserable with all the dirty looks. I had gone from a group of great friends to being a social pariah. Thank goodness it mostly stayed there, well except for the finding a date to Homecoming part. I'm hoping that's temporary, though. Those girls just happened to tell all their friends and then it snowballed and I don't know which guys know and which guys don't. Not that I'm going to give up on dating or anything. Madison is not taking that away from me."

I felt like I had to empathize with the horrible situation Julia was going through. I had pretty much been in the exact same place with Ariel, "That's almost worse than what my ex-best friend has done to me since we've stopped being friends."

"Who's your ex-best friend?" Julia asked.

"Ariel Walker," I said without thinking, totally involved in our conversation of bashing our ex-best friends.

"You were friends with Ariel Walker? Really?" Julia seemed incredulous at that fact.

I felt sort of off put by how surprised Julia sounded that Ariel and I had once been friends, "Well, yeah, up to the start of freshman year..."

"Wow," Julia shook her head, "Sorry, but I can totally see why that friendship imploded."

I had liked Julia at first and really empathized with her plight regarding Madison, but now she was staring at me like she thought Ariel's and mine friendship break-up had totally been my fault. Suddenly, I didn't like Julia so much. Did I look like some kind of a freak to her or something? I mean, I knew the rumors, but here we were having a totally normal conversation and now she was insulting me in a roundabout way. It was kind of weird. It definitely made me wonder if there was more to Madison's side of the whole Julia/Madison story than

Julia was telling me. Like maybe Madison didn't have such an ugly personality layer and Julia was embellishing on it.

I tried to be polite to Julia regardless of how I was suddenly feeling about her, which was suspicious and angry, "Well, yeah. I actually don't want to talk about it. There's more to the story than just me being a freak, I promise. No matter what Ariel tells people. I have photographic proof if I ever wanted to use it."

I added that last sentence in for effect. I wished there was some kind of proof, but there wasn't. Our friendship just fell apart.

Julia nodded, hesitated, and then said, "Well, have you thought that Ariel might have done it?"

I was confused. "Done what?"

Julia looked at me like I was a total idiot, "Killed Madison."

My brain froze as the question - Did Ariel kill Madison Brown? filled my brain. The answer my brain fired back with after it recovered from the shock was a resounding - Absolutely not! No way! And, then I started to think about it. Ariel was friends with Madison, at least sort of, but what would her motive have been? She had no reason to kill Madison. Julia, who was watching me react to this startling news, with an amused look on her face, had way more of a personal reason to kill Madison.

"Why would you say that?" I managed to ask as my brain started processing thoughts again. "As much as I don't like Ariel anymore, I don't think she could murder someone. She had no reason to kill Madison."

"Are you sure about that?" Julia asked, almost sarcastically.

I was definitely becoming less and less of a Julia fan by the moment. At first, she had come off all nice and sweet and I had empathized with her since we had both lost our best friends to horrible situations. Besides, Julia still had braces as a senior and that really sucked, but now Julia was insinuating that I was weird and that Ariel was a murderer. Even as Ariel's ex-best friend, I felt I had to defend her against that accusation.

"I know Ariel pretty well," I said adamantly, "Even if we aren't friends anymore."

"Okay," Julia smirked, "Then why don't you ask Ariel what she was doing coming out of the bathroom just before Casey Hunt went in there and found Madison Brown dead?"

My brain froze again, pondering what Julia had just said. I think my mouth dropped open too. Julia didn't give me a chance to recover either. Seemingly happy with totally flooring me, she left the bathroom.

A moment later, I made my way back to the lunchroom almost forgetting to worry what people would think about the giant wet stain that was now my shirt because my mind was on Ariel. I totally forgot about it, though, when I got back to my lunch table and noticed the table that Julia had sat down at in my absence. Despite her self-claimed pariah status, Julia was sitting at the popular table, specifically, Ethan's table, right next to him, almost too close to him.

Wait, was this a coincidence? Was Julia trying to get her status back by going after Ethan? Or, was Julia trying to throw me, personally, multiple curve balls starting with Ariel and moving on to Ethan? Who was this girl?

Ethan was looking at Julia, surprised at how close she was sitting to him when she didn't have to be. I saw the side of his face and wanted him to turn all the way around to look at me, so that I could warn him about the poisonous snake that was getting ready to wrap herself around him and go in for the kill.

CHAPTER 9
JEALOUSY SEETHING

I had to force myself to bolt out of the lunchroom as soon as the bell rang so that I wouldn't run over to Ethan and rip Julia away from him. What was Julia even playing at? I really didn't get her. One minute she was sweet, the other she was going after Ethan and proving Madison's accusations about boy stealing right even though Julia was telling me about that and denying it all in the same breath. I was getting the distinct impression that Julia enjoyed toying with people. Why did she want to toy with me? Was I an easy target? Or maybe she was afraid I'd figure out she was the murderer? Then again, maybe she was just evil. Okay, maybe there was more to her and Madison's friendship breakup than just the Pep Club presidency. I knew from firsthand experience how complicated a bff or an ex-bff relationship could be. Regardless, Julia was most definitely a piece of work and I was going to have a major problem distinguishing what was true and what was not in her story.

At least I felt better knowing that Ethan hadn't even been paying much attention to Julia during lunch. Believe me, Julia tried to get him to notice her. He just wasn't having it. That fact made me feel a little better. Not a lot better, but still. It helped curb the jealousy a little since it looked like even if Ethan was mad at me, he wasn't just going to jump into Julia's arms because she was ready and waiting. That was the Ethan I knew. Well, and I hoped that Ethan was already leaning toward forgiving me when I figured out how to apologize to him.

I had to find Ariel. I didn't want to talk to her, being that she was spreading gossip about me again, but I had to ask her about what Julia had said. I was reluctant to believe Julia because she seemed to be a total barracuda intent on catching Ethan just to get at me (or maybe also because he was hot and popular), but I couldn't ignore it either. If Julia's story was true and Ariel had been in the bathroom just before Madison's body was found, it was too sensational to ignore and Ariel had to have something to say about the accusation. A kernel of worry started forming in my stomach. I still cared about Ariel deep down even if we weren't friends.

I made a detour to try and catch Ariel at her locker before my next class. I had a general idea of where she was at all times, scarily enough, just so I could try and avoid her. It was a necessary evil. I made it just in time. Ariel was shutting her locker when I saw her. I had to ask. I took a deep breath and ran toward her before she could take more than a couple of steps away from her locker.

"Ariel!" I yelled and had a brief flashback to the first day of freshman year. When I got to school that first day, I sought Ariel out at her locker and we talked about how exciting and cool high school was going to be. Sigh, so much for that potential future.

Ariel turned, smiling, and then saw me. Her smile turned into a frown. She considered walking forward, I could tell, but turned around to face me instead. She knew I could be relentless if I truly wanted to talk to her. Ariel was getting it over with. We were sort of the same in that respect since it's how I usually felt about talking to her.

"What?" Ariel asked as I walked up to her.

"I just talked to Julia Morgan," I said, watching for Ariel's response.

"So?" Ariel asked, not seeming to care.

"She said that you walked out of the bathroom at the Homecoming Dance just before Casey Hunt found Madison dead," I said softly. Ariel might like to spread gossip, but I didn't.

"What?" Ariel practically yelled it.

Ariel took note of all the people that suddenly turned to stare at us, grabbed my arm, and dragged me down the hallway into the semi-private shelter of a closed back classroom door. It occurred to me as Ariel did this that maybe I should be scared that she was going to murder me, but I was more annoyed at how hard she was gripping my arm. I was going to have a bruise. I guess I really didn't think Ariel did it. Still, it was a bad thing if Ariel was at the scene of the crime when it happened or just after.

Ariel could still be accused and charged. The wrong person went to jail all the time in the movies, so I knew it could happen. Like, in that movie with Harrison Ford, *The Fugitive*, where he's accused of killing his wife and has to find the killer before the cops catch him. Although, I couldn't really see Ariel on the run - she's so not the kind of girl that could hide out in the woods and rough it. She'd need to toughen up and become a hardened woman like in that movie *Double Jeopardy* with Ashley Judd where she's accused of killing her husband and sentenced to jail, only he isn't actually dead, so she sets out to really kill him. Still, she wasn't guilty the first time around. Actually, I hoped it didn't come to any of that for Ariel. All of those situations made life way too complicated.

Ariel turned to face me and I could see that she was terrified, "Who told you that? Who told you I was in the bathroom?"

"Julia Morgan," I said again.

Ariel frowned, "I don't know a Julia Morgan. I don't think."

"She seems to know you," I said.

I summed it up for Ariel. Ariel was looking at me blankly. I could see she was trying to figure something out.

"Well, I don't know her, know her," Ariel said, "She wasn't in Pep Club this year at all. She must have dropped it at the end of last year or something, but I do remember some Pep Club people talking about her. I bet you she was just jealous that Madison and I were friends and she wasn't anymore. I really don't know her. Madison never even talked about her to me."

"But is it true? Did you walk out of the bathroom just before Casey Hunt walked in?" I asked.

Ariel looked at me and I could see the answer in her eyes. Oh no. Julia wasn't a complete liar.

"No," Ariel lied.

I ignored her answer, "Ariel, look, someone saw you go out of the bathroom that night. I don't know if it was Julia or if Casey said something and now it's getting around school or if it was the murderer, but anybody might have seen you. You have to tell the police before they think you're involved.""No," Ariel whispered. "I can't."

"Yes, you can," I said adamantly. "They're going to

find out."

"No," Ariel said flatly.

I sighed, feeling exasperated. Ariel wasn't going to listen to me. There was nothing I could do. I had to take a different tactic.

"Well did you see anything?" I asked.

"No," Ariel said.

"Ariel, come on," I tried again.

"What? I didn't see anything," Ariel's voice cracked on the last word.

"Ariel. Please. Help me. Did you see anything?" I pleaded. "I'm not going to tell anyone. I'm just looking for a lead."

Ariel hesitated, "Fine. I was in the bathroom with Madison before she died. We went in together to fix our make-up. She was having hair issues that wouldn't resolve themselves and it was taking her forever. I was done and I wanted to get back out to Troy and dance, so I left her in there. I did pass Casey on my way out. We actually stopped to talk outside the bathroom. I didn't have blood on me or anything, I swear. I didn't kill her. Casey will tell you. Troy will tell you that too. I didn't do it."

"How long did you stop to talk to Casey?" I asked, as I felt the ball of dread in my stomach start growing. Ariel had been at the scene of the crime within minutes of the murder, maybe seconds. That wasn't good.

Ariel shrugged, "A few minutes. I mean, we were telling each other how great we looked and bragging about our dates. Casey was trying to one up me, but there was no way she was going to one up me going to the dance with a college guy. You know?"

"Could anyone have walked past you guys and into the bathroom while you were talking?" I asked.

Ariel shrugged, "I didn't notice anyone, but my back

was to the bathroom. Casey would probably have been the one to notice that. So, maybe, but I didn't notice. I mean, we were talking so..."

"Did you hear anything?" I asked. "When you were talking to Casey? Like a struggle? Anything?"

"No," Ariel said. "Nothing."

"So, you were literally the last person to see Madison alive besides the murderer?" I asked. This looked so bad.

Ariel turned pale, "Yes. But, the thing is, I think there might have been someone else in one of the stalls. I wasn't thinking about it at the time. It was just Madison and I talking at the bathroom sink when I left, but I'd almost swear there was someone in a stall. I think."

"That's huge! Can you remember any detail? Like their shoes? You can usually see shoes under the stall. Did you see them?" I asked, thinking rapidly.

Ariel was freaking out, realizing that maybe she had seen something of the killer and what that meant. Ariel didn't hear my question or didn't want to answer it and just said, "What if they heard me talking? What if that person knows who I am and decides to murder me too because they think I saw them? I can't talk about it. Nobody can know."

I grabbed Ariel by the arms and looked at her in all seriousness, "Ariel, what did you see?"

Ariel's eyes were worried, but she whispered, "I saw red Chuck Taylor high tops with black and white striped laces. I remember thinking that some weird girl had to be in the bathroom wearing chucks to the Homecoming Dance. That's the only reason I noticed. I thought it might be you actually, but..."

I frowned at Ariel, "And, you're sure it was a girl? Could it have been a guy?"

Ariel looked at me, like she hadn't even considered the

gender change, "Maybe it could have been a guy. I mean, I wasn't thinking in that direction. I just thought it was some punk rock girl or something. I guess it could have been a guy, if his pants were high. I don't remember legs. I just saw the red of the chucks. The stalls are kind of low, though, so I could have just missed the legs. I don't know."

I took this in. This was a huge clue. I looked down at my own black Chuck Taylors. Thank goodness I stuck to the classic color of black in this case and I actually hadn't worn mine to the dance. I had gone all out and worn heels, even though they made me feel rickety.

If only Ariel could have told me about the legs. I knew what she meant about the school bathroom stalls, though. They were low. Like, you could easily look over them low if you wanted to because the teachers needed to be able to look into the stalls if they, say, smelled something that wasn't legal emanating from a stall and to discourage making out in one. The doors thus, were oddly low to the ground. Like it mattered if people could see your feet if they could already see a lot more if they looked over the bathroom stall wall.

"Don't tell anyone, okay?" Ariel was pleading with me.

"I won't," I said, although I wasn't sure it would matter if the gossip had already started spreading that Ariel was the last one to see Madison alive.

The bell rang, startling both of us. Ariel and I looked at each other in panic and bolted in opposite directions for our classes.

CHAPTER 10
MIND TURNING

I was in no mood to pay attention to teachers for the rest of the day. First off, Ethan and apologizing to him was totally on my mind. And, then, interjecting into those thoughts were their polar opposites. I kept going over the details and suspects in Madison's murder and over Ariel's confession at seeing the potential killer's shoes.

I had taken no notes in any of my classes since lunch, so I was glad when the bell rang. I hoped the teachers hadn't said anything too important and that most of it wouldn't be on any tests. If it was, I'd be failing that test and my grades were already probably going to take a hit if I didn't finish all the make-up work I had to get done. The teachers were relentless, even though I had a valid excuse, like being in the hospital. They didn't care. Homework was homework and the general gist was, in the real world you'd have to get the work done, blah, blah, blah.

Speaking of the real world, I was heading straight from school to my job at Palos Video Store. I hadn't been back since I had been shot there. My boss, Anne, had ended up in the hospital too, but she had completely recovered. Luckily, there hadn't been much damage to the store in the shooting and after the police crime scene tape came down, it opened right back up like nothing had ever happened. Anne couldn't even afford for it to close for a day with the current competition of Netflix, Red Box, Blockbuster, etc. cutting into her DVD and Blu-ray rental profits. Almost as a blessing, business spiked after the incident. Ethan told me that the parking lot was packed every afternoon when he drove by it on the way to visit me at the hospital. It was all the free press and curiosity seekers reminding people that the store was still there. I guess that's what people meant when they said the phrase - a blessing in disguise. It was a good thing. I liked my job at Palos Video Store. I wanted to keep it at least through high school, so it had to stay open.

I walked in right on time. I had been a little flakey a couple weeks before and I wanted to impress upon Anne my commitment to doing my job. She was in the back watching a movie when I got there. I hadn't seen her since the whole shooting debacle and things felt a bit awkward.

"Hey," I managed. It was a normal thing to say to your boss, right? I just wanted things to be normal, at work, at the very least.

"Hey," Anne said, looking up from her movie, *Before Sunrise*. She mostly stayed in the back and supervised the employees unless we got really busy and then she ran up front to help. It was the perk of owning the place and everyone thought she was a cool boss so it didn't matter, "You okay?"

"Yeah," I nodded, feeling a cold sweat come on. I couldn't help but feel that Anne ending up in the hospital was half my fault. I had led a killer straight to us. "You?"

Anne nodded, "Took a few days, but much better."

"Good," I said and not knowing what to say commented on the movie she was watching, "Ethan

Hawke is cute."

Of course, just saying the name Ethan made me think of my Ethan. My heart hurt. It couldn't be over between us. It had barely just started.

Anne nodded, not noticing that my head was already not in the conversation, "This movie is one of my comfort food movies. You just watch them talk about life for two hours. It's great."

I smiled, "Yeah... I should go up front."

I left Anne to watch her movie. I had my own things to think about and talk over in my head or better yet, avoid thinking about. I walked over to the counter and set down my bag. I felt like getting out my ereader and reading for fun to try and push out the Ethan thoughts, but I had too big of a mound of homework to finish to even consider that. I pulled out my Chemistry book and a worksheet I had to complete. I vaguely wished Kyle had let me copy his. I was all about learning, but I had a billion worksheets to make up. It was going to take me forever. I sighed and started on the first question.

It took me almost the entire night to finish the one worksheet. I could never afford to miss school again. I still had current homework from other classes to finish when I got home, not to mention my murder investigation work. I wondered if I should call Ethan. He hadn't tried to call me or anything. Not that I blamed him. I was the one that had messed up. It had been hours and I still couldn't think of a way to apologize. What was wrong with me? Why was I avoiding this? I couldn't wait much longer or Ethan might think I wasn't sorry. Did he already think that? I looked at my phone. I only had about thirty minutes until the store closed.

I'd call Ethan as soon as I got into my car after work. I couldn't let him think that I wasn't sorry. I just... No, I had to do it. Ethan was important to me. I had to say I was sorry to him and then I could expound on it and make it a huge apology as I went along. I wasn't beneath groveling. I had totally disregarded my promise to him. The fight was completely my fault. Yet, there was a small part of me that felt like looking into this mystery was something that I had to do. I pushed that away. No, my promise to Ethan should have been more important.

Just as I was thinking that I couldn't wait for work to be over so I could get all this Ethan thinking off my brain, I heard someone walk into the store. I froze and had a weird deja vu flashback. Ethan had walked into the store. It was just like the first time he walked into my life. I felt giddy and nervous and I didn't know what to do.

"I'm so sorry," I gushed and walked around the corner of the cashier counter toward him, not caring if Anne heard my blithering apology to Ethan.

Ethan walked toward me, "I'm sorry too. I shouldn't have made you promise. It wasn't fair of me to do that. I..."

Then suddenly we were kissing in the middle of the store. It was like a romantic movie moment in any of those great movies like *Titanic* or *Gone With the Wind* or *Pride and Prejudice* or *Sixteen Candles*. It was just me and Ethan and the kissing.

I heard Anne clear her throat and I jumped away from Ethan, guiltily.

"I'm so sorry, Anne," I said, feeling my cheeks burning bright red. This was so unlike me to make out with a guy at work. Oh, who was I kidding? This was really the first opportunity I had to do that and I totally went for it. I just couldn't believe I had done it at work. I had such good intentions when I got there to do nothing scandalous or flaky, but so much for good intentions.

Anne looked between us and frowned trying not to crack a smile, "Just wait until your shift is over."

I nodded and whispered to Ethan, "See you in twenty."

Ethan grinned and walked out of the store. I went back to the counter and packed up my things. Homework was over for the night. All I could think about was kissing Ethan. After about a minute, my thoughts returned back to normal. Was our fight over? Who won? Was it okay if I continued investigating the murder? Or, by kissing Ethan had I told him my promise to not investigate was back on? I was really confused. Was this a we need to talk moment? Because I kind of dreaded saying those words to Ethan.

Anne told me to leave about five minutes early. I was done with all the usual close up tasks and pacing, waiting for Anne to pack up and leave the store with me, like was the norm for closing. I think I was getting too antsy for Anne to take. I grabbed my bag and forced myself not to run out of the store. Ethan didn't need to know how eager slash nervous I was, after all. It was important that I act totally normal.

I walked out of the store and saw Ethan's car parked on the street, a little ways down. I left my car in the parking lot and walked to his and knocked on his window. He unlocked his doors and I got into the car, feeling suddenly first date nervous.

"Hey," I said automatically and then felt stupid.

Ethan smiled and leaned in toward me. Then we were kissing again. I could totally get used to this making up after an argument thing. It was totally amazing and awesome and great. I'd even give up Wired's peanut butter banana milkshakes if it meant this could last longer. And, then suddenly I was pulling away from

Ethan. What was wrong with me?

"Um," I managed, my brain trying to assemble its thoughts into a cohesive statement, "Where do we stand on the whole investigating Madison's murder issue?"

Ethan looked at me blankly like he didn't understand what I was saying at first. Wow, did me kissing him have that effect on him too? I felt a giddy happiness in my stomach, but it quickly disappeared as I started worrying about why Ethan wasn't answering my question.

"So?" I prodded.

"Uh," Ethan ran a hand through his hair. It was great hair, but I stopped myself from running my hands through it and getting both of us distracted. Ethan took a ragged breath. "I'm not thrilled with the whole investigating thing, but..."

I could take a but! What was the but? Ethan was hesitating again, like he was deciding something.

"But what?" I asked.

Ethan frowned at me, "But I'd like to investigate with you."

I was surprised. That was so not something negative. I'd rather have Ethan on the case with me, holding my hand, stealing kisses, making out in parked cars. Oh wait, we didn't need to be investigating a case to do that. I smiled.

Ethan smiled back at me and I felt a weight lift off of my chest, "You can be like my sidekick."

Ethan's smile quickly turned into a frown, "What about partner?"

I smiled at him, feeling silly. "Nah, sidekick. Definitely sidekick."

Ethan looked at me sideways, studying me and then I saw the corners of his mouth turn up wryly, "You want me to be a wacky sidekick, don't you?"

"Yeah," I grinned. "That would be pretty great."

Ethan looked at me.

"What?" I asked.

"Should I wear a costume?" Ethan asked.

"Sure!" I said, thinking of all the cute Ethan costume sidekick possibilities. There was something adorable about the thought of seeing him in a cape like a superhero or a trench coat like Mulder and Scully wore in *The X-Files*.

"Okay. So, just one more thing then: What's the pay for a good sidekick these days?" Ethan asked as seriously as he could, but I could tell he was trying not to smile.

"Kisses!" I said, taking the bait, and leaned in toward him.

Ethan laughed and kissed me back and then pulled away to look at me, "So, where are you in the investigation anyway?"

I recapped all of what I knew so far to Ethan. I was glad when he stopped me to claim that even he had thought Julia Morgan coming onto him was really weird because he had never talked to her before and that, just in case I wanted to know, he was not at all interested in her. Good.

Other than that, Ethan listened and nodded in all the right places and didn't distract me with kissing even once. At least, not until after I was done giving him all the details.

As we broke off from kissing again, Ethan looked at me seriously. "So, you still haven't talked to Casey Hunt, then?"

"No," I said. "She hasn't been at school. I heard she was out sick."

"I think I can get to her," Ethan said.

"Really?" I asked. "How?"

Ethan shrugged, "We used to date."

I felt my stomach drop out from under me. I had just been feeling so confident and un-jealous about our dating relationship. That was fast. Now my stomach was churning wearily.

I didn't know that Ethan had dated Casey. Where was I when that happened? I mean, I hadn't been stalking him or anything, but surely I would have heard they were going out if they had been an item.

"When did you date her?" I asked.

"Freshman year," Ethan said, "But we're cool now. I have a plan."

I was definitely not going to like this plan. I was not going to like it at all. Not even one little bit. My stomach hurt. No, I was so not going to like this plan, even if I knew that we had to talk to Casey Hunt to move forward in the investigation. Maybe I really should have dropped the case instead of having Ethan join me in murder solving. We didn't really need to talk to Casey did we?

CHAPTER 11
EAVESDROPPING

I didn't sleep well. Then I got up early to try and look extra good for meeting up with Casey Hunt after school. Well, the looking good part was actually for Ethan, but I also wanted to look amazing standing next to Casey, or at least my very best attempt at looking amazing. It was a bit of a disaster instead. I tried to curl my hair and ended up with some burnt hair. It smelled totally bad. Then when I made myself some maple brown sugar oatmeal, I spilled some on myself, so I had to change my shirt. I really was not having luck with keeping food off of my clothes lately. It was not a good morning. I hoped my luck would turn by the time Ethan and I met up with Casey.

On the bus on my way to school, I looked over my investigation notebook. Besides wanting to talk to Casey and keeping my eyes open for anyone - guy or girl - wearing red high top Chuck Taylors, I also wanted to talk to Madison's date to the dance, Sebastian Zane. I wasn't sure how that was going to happen, even though I knew what he looked like from a quick glance at my yearbook this morning. I just had no idea where to run into him or if I did, how to approach him. After my run-ins with Noah and Julia, I was kind of weary of talking to anyone in the student body about the murder.

I got to school about ten minutes before the bell was going to ring for first period. I threw the books I didn't need into my locker and got out the ones I did and decided to walk the halls looking for Sebastian. It couldn't hurt. I could decide if I wanted to talk to him or not after I found him.

I was busy walking randomly down a hallway near where my Chemistry class was on my search, when I heard it. I didn't normally follow gossip, but my ears caught this piece and took it in.

"And, I can't believe that Julia Morgan swept in and became Pep Club President. It's just so unfair. She hasn't even been to any of the meetings this year even if her name is on the roster," a girl with long black hair was saying to her friend.

"Why? Did you want to be President?" her friend with a short pixie cut and flaming red hair asked.

The black haired girl paused, "Yeah, you know, I would. It's my senior year. I've been to every meeting and yeah, I mean, it would look good on my college applications. I might have been the next in line for it. I know Madison would never have wanted Julia to take over for her. I might have to quit now. I hate Julia. She totally went after Paul last year. This totally sucks."

I had to keep walking, but I really wanted to pay more attention to their conversation. I glanced around, but there was nowhere within earshot for me to hang around near the two girls gossiping without being noticed. In addition, the crowd of students was rapidly thinning out since the five minute warning bell was about to ring to signal that students should get to their classes. So I kept walking, my brain flying with thoughts.

Julia had gotten the Pep Club Presidency just like she'd wanted. It was definitely a plus for her that Madison was out of the way. I'd also admit that Julia hadn't left the best impression on me with the way she'd decided to torment me by coming onto Ethan at lunch the day before. I could definitely see why she and Madison might have stopped being friends in the first place.

The warning bell rang and brought me out of my thoughts. I headed to my first class, still not having found Sebastian. I'd keep looking for him and anyone with red Chuck Taylor high tops. So far black ones seemed the most popular, though. That was good, since it meant if I found someone with red high tops, they might actually be the killer. Or they'd be a really good witness, at the very least. Still, with the short time window Ariel had given me, it was looking like Red High Tops was the only person who would have had the time and access to kill Madison.

My classes until lunch flew by. Kyle and Suzie shot each other goo-goo eyes all of Chemistry and I tried to ignore them. They were almost too gushy at this point. I sure hoped Ethan and I weren't like this. Just the thought of Ethan, though, made me wish it was already lunchtime. I wanted to see him! It hadn't even been twenty-four hours and I was already craving his presence. What was wrong with me? Maybe Ethan and I were just as grossly lovey-dovey as Kyle and Suzie. Oh well. I was a happy hypocrite.

I felt a little nervous walking into lunch. I didn't want either Noah or Julia to join Ethan and I at lunch today. I still wondered if Ethan was weary about me investigating Madison's murder despite what he said the night before in the car. I would understand it if he was still bothered by it. I mean, Liz's death wasn't that long ago and it had to bring up some unhappy thoughts. I hoped Ethan knew he could talk to me about it.

Then I worried if Ethan would actually sit with me at lunch again. We hadn't actually discussed it. And, it had never been a permanent thing. The thing was, I didn't relish sitting alone at lunch anymore. Prior to Ethan I had enjoyed the time alone, using the lunch hour to read or finish homework, but it was much more fun to hang out at lunch and talk to Ethan than eat cheese fries by myself and read a book.

I felt a huge wave of relief wash over me as I saw that Ethan was already sitting at my lunch table, waiting for me. I had to act normal, though. I couldn't let him know he affected me like this.

I walked up to him and set down my books, "Hey."

Ethan looked up from his sandwich, "Hey."

I walked to the lunch line and started breathing again. I still felt like things were on tender hooks. I knew we had just made up from our fight only the night before and that technically we weren't anything yet anyway, but it just felt like so much was at stake even with simple word exchanges. Did all relationships feel like this? I quickly grabbed a healthy slice of pizza and a pop and hurried back to Ethan.

All it took was those five minutes for the whole school day to change. I was barely at my lunch table when the intercom buzzed on.

"Classes, after school activities, and sports are cancelled for today. Busses will be waiting outside shortly," The principal said.

My mind shorted out. The last time we had been forced to leave the school someone had been murdered. I walked to Ethan in a daze. He stared at me with what I thought was a similar expression. Had it really happened again?

"It sounds like someone died," I said, speaking my

thoughts aloud.

Ethan nodded as if in slow motion, "I just heard it was Julia Morgan."

CHAPTER 12
EX-GIRLFRIEND CONNING

Even though Julia had made a bad impression on me, I would not have wished her dead. This was insane. Two people in the span of days, both killed while they were technically in school. I wouldn't blame people for starting to ditch at this point. You might be safer in an out of school suspension, at home, or out on the town. The murderer definitely had to be someone in the student body. Well, unless it was a faculty member or a parent.

Ethan and I were forced to toss out our lunches without eating much of them. We quickly made plans to meet at 3:30 pm and carry out our plan to talk to Casey Hunt, despite the insanity of the day's events. I wanted to ride the bus home and listen to the gossip, actually. Even if the faculty said nothing, the other students might know what happened to Julia. It now seemed even more imperative that our investigation continued. In fact, we needed to hurry up and find the murderer before they killed someone else.

According to the gossip I heard running rampant on the bus, this was what happened to Julia. She had been seen in her first two classes, bragging about the Pep Club

Presidency. Well, only one girl said that on the bus, but I'm sure it was true. Then just before first lunch hour, Julia got a pass and she went five minutes down the street to pick up a bunch of cupcakes some mom baked for a Pep Club bake sale that had been organized to happen at lunch. It was Julia's first duty as president and her only duty. Julia never made it back to school because the brake lines in her car had been cut and she careened into a brick wall. Of course, I'm sure the police were still investigating the exact cause of the collision and it hadn't been ruled a murder yet. The school, with another tragedy, had gone by the books and cancelled classes. The two deaths were totally connected, of that, I was sure. Why else would two Pep Club presidents die within the span of days? Someone definitely didn't have school spirit.

I was having trouble processing the fact that Julia was dead even though I didn't much like her. I was probably in shock. I knew the whole school had to be. The obvious secondary connection between the two girls was that they had been best friends at some point. I wondered which connection - the Pep Club presidency or their friendship was the important common link. Unless, of course, I was missing some information and there was another connection. Still, I wouldn't be rearing to become Pep Club president anytime soon. It seemed like it was turning out to be a deadly job.

I was home at a little after 1:30 pm. That gave me about two hours before Ethan came to pick me up. I spent the time touching up my hair and makeup and doing some online research. I glanced at old Facebook posts between Julia and Madison and they seemed like they had been really good friends, until they completely stopped being friends, even on Facebook. I looked at their friends in common, but that was really no help.

They were both friends with half the school. It was too many people for me to weed through if we hoped to find the killer anytime in the next six months, much less the next few days. Besides, they might not be friends with the killer. Oh, who was I kidding, it could be anyone. I was still gunning for Red High Tops, though.

Then I checked out the Pep Club group page for Palos High School that had been set up. It had a little over a hundred online members. Somehow, I was betting not all of these people actually showed up to meetings. I recognized a few names like Ariel and about ten people I went to class with, but I didn't know a lot of the others. I took note that Madison's date to the dance, Sebastian Zane, made an appearance on the list. Maybe Pep Club was the way to find him, although he might be totally irrelevant now, since there had been a second girl murdered that wasn't his date to the dance. Still, it couldn't hurt to talk to him if I got the chance.

As I scrolled through the members of Pep Club my thought was that in general, they really seemed like one happy and cheery bunch. Of course, it couldn't be all true if someone was murdering them, well, unless that person really did have a vendetta against school spirit. I mean, could the answers to these murders be as simple as an anti-high school psycho or misfit? Maybe, but so far, in my experience, I'd guess at something more personal.

I definitely needed to re-up my Pep Club membership and go to a meeting and not just for my college transcripts either. Maybe not all of these people were as happy and cheery as they seemed to be. There sure seemed to be a lot more to Madison and Julia than met the eye. I put it on my list of things to do. Between investigating murders, work, and my pile of homework, not to mention time kissing Ethan, I was going to be a busy girl.

Ethan showed up promptly at 3:30 pm. He had changed clothes and was wearing dress pants and a button down shirt. I looked down at my t-shirt and jeans and wondered if I too should have dressed up to talk to Casey Hunt. I mean, it was a cute t-shirt, but nothing dressy.

"Not at all," Ethan said and then smiled sheepishly, "When we were dating, Casey always used to try to get me to dress up. This is a buttering up technique."

I wasn't sure that I liked the thought of Ethan using his hotness to butter up another girl that wasn't me, but since he knew Casey best, I'd have to take his lead - at least, for now.

Casey lived about five minutes from my house and we were already there before I could get really nervous about this plan. Besides, my brain was still going over the facts of Julia's murder and who I might want to talk to about it. Truthfully, the whole school had access to the parking lot and anybody could have stepped outside for a quick brake line cutting if they really wanted. Still, it was good that I was preoccupied. I could be thinking about other things - like being jealous that Casey used to date Ethan.

"Are you ready?" Ethan asked, getting out of the car in front of Casey's house.

I nodded, even though my stomach was full of freaked out butterflies. We could do this. I could do this. Although, Ethan was actually the one who had the toughest job ahead of him. Well, I was hoping it was going to be at least a little hard for him to talk to Casey, being that they were exes and all.

Ethan walked up to the front door, while I walked around the corner and watched from behind some bushes and a tall oak tree. I hoped nobody would think I was scouting the house out to rob it or something. I saw the door to the house open and after saying something I couldn't hear, Ethan walked inside. He was in. All was going according to plan so far.

I was supposed to wait ten minutes. The ten minutes felt like eons. Ethan thought he was anxious when I had gone off with Troy during our last murder investigation together. That was nothing compared to stamping approval on letting Ethan go off into a house with his ex-girlfriend for ten minutes. My brain kept wanting to imagine what might be happening with the two of them. Nothing, I kept telling myself. Nothing was happening except talking and Ethan conning Casey, well, sort of - most of that part was up to me.

I tried not to run toward Casey Hunt's house when my alarm went off at the ten minute mark. I forced myself to walk calmly up the steps. I took a deep breath, preparing to go into character, glad for once at my insane reputation.

I started banging on the door like there was no tomorrow. I tried not to feel bad for what I was about to do. Ethan had assured me that this was the only way to get Casey to talk to us. Otherwise, I'd feel a little bad at conning a girl who had just gone through a really traumatic event.

The door flew open and I almost fell forward with the force of how hard I had just been banging on the door.

"Is Ethan Ripley here?!?!?" I yelled, like I had gone totally insane.

Casey Hunt looked back at me, face white with shock.

I tried not to let it bother me, "Is Ethan here? Because his car is out front and if he is, he needs to explain to me what he is doing at some other girl's house when he's my boyfriend and... Well, is he here?"

Casey definitely didn't know what to do. I could see the war raging in her head - did she tell this psycho girl that yes, Ethan was in her bedroom or did she lie?

"Uh, no, actually..." Casey started, choosing the lie, hoping I'd believe it.

"Really? Because his car is right in front of your house," I stared Casey down, daring her to challenge me again.

I saw Casey glance at Ethan's car, which was very obviously parked right in front of her house. Casey looked back at me and I could tell that she didn't know what to do.

"Well?" I said. "You want to tell me why his car is in front of your house if he's not inside?"

Casey sighed, relenting, "Yes, he's here, but seriously nothing is going on. It's a long story, but..."

"I need to see him," I interrupted her.

Casey was totally caught off guard, "Yeah, sure. Uh, follow me."

Casey walked up the stairs and her room was the first door on the right. She kept looking back at me nervously, like she was having major second thoughts about letting me into her house instead of just calling the police. Ethan was sitting on her bed. I tried not to feel jealous. It wasn't a pleasant sight for me to see, so this whole acting thing was not going to be too hard.

"Ethan Ripley, what are you doing here?" I asked. I felt like I went a little over the top, though, by using his full name. I saw Ethan raise his eyebrows. So much for thinking this acting thing was easy.

I snuck a glance at Casey as she was looking at Ethan, who was doing his best to appear guilty and surprised. At least Casey seemed to be buying the whole charade. That was good. Ethan's whole theory was that Casey would be super glad to see him, which was good in that she might confide her feelings to him, but bad because she'd probably be more likely to try and make-out with him. So, I was there to put the kibosh on a make-out session and get Casey to talk because Ethan had spent ten minutes consoling her. I glanced at him eyes narrowed, that was all that better have been happening. Wow, I was getting great at being in character!

"I'm just here to talk to Casey about Madison. I wanted to make sure Casey was alright," Ethan said and then added, "I swear."

I believed Ethan and felt the ball of tension building in my stomach disappear, but I looked at him unsurely anyway. Let him worry. Then, I looked at Casey with raised eyebrows.

"Oh, yeah," I paused, trying my best to sound instantly sympathetic instead of the angry girl I had been seconds ago, "You found Madison, right? Are you okay?"

Casey looked suddenly teary as if all of this talking about the murder and her finding a dead body was finally getting to her, but nodded, "Yeah. It was just so awful."

"I'm so sorry," I said and I meant it. It had to be awful to find a dead body.

Casey nodded, "Yeah. Thanks."

I put a hand on her shoulder, sympathetically, "What happened?"

Then it just spilled out of Casey. She must have been dying to talk to somebody, "It was so freaky. I mean, I was walking into the bathroom and I saw Ariel, you know, Ariel Walker? And, we stopped to talk. Then I walked into the bathroom. I really had to pee. I had like three Diet Cokes and I pushed open the stall and there she was...dead. I just keep thinking if I hadn't pushed open that stall..."

"Wow," I interrupted before Casey could get off track and then asked, "Like, how was she dead?"

"Someone had shot her," Casey replied.

"Wow," I said again, thinking that the gossipmongers had been embellishing the murder with their talk of a *Kill Bill* style scene.

Shooting someone in the middle of a dance worked, though. With or without a silencer, the noise from the dance would probably drown the whole thing out. Or, people would assume it was part of the beat of the song.

Casey nodded, "Yeah, but definitely dead. It was insane. I know Ariel had just walked out, but I don't think she did it at all or anything. Really. I told the police that too."

"Why not?" I asked.

Casey looked at me, "Because she's Ariel Walker. She's beautiful, popular, and she has a college guy boyfriend."

I wasn't sure those reasons would be enough for the police to not think of Ariel as a suspect, much less a judge or jury. I hoped it wouldn't come to that.

"Anything else?" I asked.

Casey hesitated, "Well, there was one more weird thing. I mean, someone had to have been in the bathroom between when Ariel left and I walked in or something. I didn't notice anybody because I was busy looking at Ariel's dress and trying to figure out the designer. Did you see her dress?"

I had seen it, but it hadn't struck me as amazing or anything. I couldn't even remember the color, "Uh, no."

"It was fantastic," Casey gushed and then went on, "Anyway, but in the bathroom when I walked in on Madison, I did notice something."

"What?" I asked.

"In the bathroom stall above her, the killer wrote - Who's peppy now?" Casey said.

Ethan and I both stared at her. This was a detail that hadn't been released to the gossips at Palos High School and it was a definite help to the case. Did it mean that the killer was simply anti-pep club? Or, maybe they just didn't share Madison's school spirit. It was an extra fact that helped set the scene. We just couldn't jump for joy at learning it until we were out of Casey's sight.

"What did you do after you found her?" I asked.

"I screamed and freaked out and ran out of the bathroom to find a teacher," Casey said. "It's kind of a blur. I couldn't stop screaming. It was horrible."

If the murderer hadn't gotten out of the bathroom before Casey walked in or escaped when Casey and Ariel were talking, the killer had another chance to get out of the bathroom after Casey found the body. I supposed they could have crawled into a vent or something too and done a disappearing act that way, but that would have definitely meant planning and premeditation since you'd need a tool to get into the vent. Still, all of this meant that it was possible the murderer had totally gone unseen and with a gunshot, they might not have had any blood on their clothes. The killer could be anyone. That wasn't good for our investigation.

"Okay, Kait, I think we've bothered Casey long enough," Ethan broke the silence.

Casey looked at Ethan longingly. I resisted the urge to pull Ethan out of the house. Casey smiled at Ethan.

"Yeah, I think you're right. I'm sorry for freaking out and banging on your door and stuff, Casey," I said and I really meant it.

Casey nodded, but I had a feeling there would be some more rumors spread about me once she went back to school. It was worth it, though.

Ethan walked over to me, but spoke to Casey, "Feel better and let me know if you need to talk or anything."

"Thanks," Casey managed a smile.

I grabbed Ethan possessively by the arm and dragged him out of the house. Casey followed us to the front door, unsuspecting, and watched us drive away. I didn't think about the weirdness of that - Ethan and I driving away together - because we had come separately to Casey's house, until we were down the street. Oh well, at least we had gotten some information out of her before Casey could start suspecting us of conning her.

When we were out of eyesight of the house, I turned to Ethan, "We got something."

"Yes, we did," Ethan said. "How do you think it fits?"

"Well, it could be a signature..." I said, thinking. "Something the killer does in all his murders."

On TV and in movies, I was sure I'd seen fictional serial killers leave signatures of sorts. Of course, this wasn't like in *Dexter* where the way the killer drained the bodies of blood the first season was the signature. Maybe this killer wrote pithy comments near their victims. Or, maybe it was just Madison. It was too bad we couldn't get a look at the writing - maybe it would tell us if the killer was more likely to be a guy or a girl. Although, somehow I couldn't picture someone who wore red chucks to the Homecoming Dance writing in bubbly letters with hearts over the i's.

Ethan nodded, "Maybe it really is all about the Pep Club."

"It definitely could be," I said. "She...or he particularly focused on Madison's peppiness for the comment. That has to mean something."

"So what next?" Ethan asked.

"How about we stop for peanut butter banana milkshakes at Wired?" I said, smiling.

"Of course," Ethan grinned back at me, "But I meant, about the murder?"

I turned my brain off of the mouthwatering thoughts of Wired's milkshakes, "Well, how do you feel about joining Pep Club with me?"

CHAPTER 13
PEP CLUB FAKING

Through Facebook, I found out that we were in luck. Pep Club was having an emergency meeting after school on Wednesday. They didn't say what the emergency was exactly, but my guess was that it had to do with the murder of two of their members and presidents in a matter of days. They were now without a student leader. I wondered who was going to step up to be the next target, er, Pep Club president.

The morning went by in a quick breeze of boring lectures, until I went to Chemistry. There I found Suzie waiting for me outside of class with one of the most good looking guys I had ever seen. I would have stopped short of them in a dead stare of shock if my brain had continued to work at the sight of them looking at me as I walked toward them. I had, of course, seen this guy in school, but we had never spoken. That being said, Ethan was still way hotter in my book, but this guy was an otherworldly super model hot. His name was Logan Collins and he was a senior, easily the most popular guy in his class. Every girl knew who he was, even if they never dared dream that he'd speak to them. How did quiet, shy girl Suzie Whitsett know him? And, what was she doing standing outside of our classroom with him? Kyle was going to freak. Logan Collins blew all guys out of the water with his hotness. Well, except Ethan...to me.

"Kait, we've been waiting for you," Suzie said.

I couldn't help, but glance at Logan. He had been waiting for me. My life had gone surreal again. I felt my cheeks turn pink. No teenage boy should have this affect on a girl just by way of his cuteness.

"Oh?" I think I said. It might have come out more like a grunt or a gurgle because my brain was still trying to process the situation.

"I wanted to talk to you," Logan said, peering at me, "Suzie said you were investigating Madison and Julia's murders? I want to help."

"You want to help?" I repeated. Again, my brain was trying to understand the words that were working to penetrate it. Wow, this guy was hot.

"Yeah, I used to know them when we were kids. We were best friends in junior high. Then we weren't, but I do feel like I know something important to your investigation. I still talked to them every once in awhile and Julia and I went to Homecoming together, actually," Logan said. "Just as friends."

I nodded. What was wrong with me? I couldn't help staring at Logan. Why had Julia complained about not having a date to the dance? Logan was the hottest guy in school, next to Ethan of course, even if they had gone to the dance as just friends. I mean, with Logan on her arm, did Julia even need to try and go after Ethan? Who was that girl anyway? Then I noticed Logan was talking again. I struggled to pay attention. This guy was so good looking it was distracting.

"I think I know who might have done it. I thought

about going to the police, but I don't really want to get involved. I mean, people here talk and I'm me, you know, but if you're looking into their deaths, maybe you could check the guy out and see if he and his friends are worth even telling the police about and if they are, tell them for me," Logan said.

I felt bewitched by Logan. His eyes were staring into mine. It was different from Ethan, though. Ethan made my stomach do flips and I mostly longed to kiss him. Logan sort of floored me and made my mind go numb. He was too handsome for his own good, for my own good. Seriously, no guy should have this sort of effect on a girl. It wasn't good for him...or the girl in question.

"Okay," I said, brain moving forward slowly, "Who do you think did it?"

"It's a hunch," Logan started, "But there's this weird guy that's been following Madison around and stalking her because she was the president of Pep Club. His name's Seth Wilcox. He and his friends are really anti school spirit and they've been giving her a hard time."

"Okay. Like what? And, how do you know about it?" I asked.

"Madison told me. We still talked sometimes. And, I kind of knew this kid from way back in junior high too. She knew that. Madison said that he and his friends had gone so far as to destroy the posters and all the decorations for the Pep Club Homecoming float. Everyone was really upset about it, but they all rallied and fixed something up in time. Madison was amazing like that - she'd just pull stuff together and make it happen the way she wanted to," Logan said.

"Did she report what happened?" I asked. "To the school? Or the police?"

"I don't know. Madison admitted to me that she was

scared, but didn't think that they'd do anything serious. Looks like maybe they did and then continued on with Julia, although I guess there's some people who think that will be ruled an accident," Logan said. "Since it was a car wreck and all."

"Everyone knows it wasn't, though," Suzie said. "So, what do you think Kait?"

"I'll check Seth Wilcox out. For sure. Thanks, Logan," I said, lingering on his name.

Logan nodded, "You're welcome. I hope you catch the guy."

"Me too," I said.

Logan waved to Suzie and walked down the hallway toward his next class. Suzie and I both watched him walk away. When Logan turned the corner, I felt like I had suddenly been set free from an enchantment and I turned to Suzie, eyes wide.

"Okay, you have to tell me. How in the world do you know Logan Collins? And, why did you keep that a secret?" I asked.

Suzie smiled, "I met him through Madison in junior high and he's been nice to me ever since. He used to be such a geek, with pimples and braces and stuff. So, he was just as shy as me. Then his mom took him to the dermatologist and the orthodontist. There were probably some genetics in there too once he hit puberty. Then bam! Logan became popular because one school year he showed up after summer vacation as super hot and all of the girls fell in love with him. Still, when I saw him, Logan would talk to me. He was cool. So, we stayed school friends. We never hung out or anything...or dated or anything."

I glanced into Chemistry class to see if Kyle had witnessed Suzie, Logan and me talking. He was already inside and looking in our direction. It was too far away to tell if he was worried that Logan was going to steal Suzie away from him. My guess is that Kyle was totally flipping out with thoughts that Suzie was running off with the most popular guy in school and that his brief moment of true love happiness was gone.

I looked at Suzie and gestured to Kyle, "Well, I'd tell Kyle that you were just school friends because I wouldn't blame him for feeling just a little bit threatened."

Suzie looked horrified at the thought and went inside to console Kyle. I looked down the hallway to where Logan had disappeared. It was totally surreal that I actually managed to form words in front of him. Then I followed Suzie into Chemistry class.

I ran to my locker after the final school bell rang to get out the last of the books I needed to finish up my make-up homework. I groaned inwardly as I realized it was still going to take me a couple more days. There was a lot left to do. I had just shut my locker door when Ethan walked up. It was nice having him meet me at my locker, almost as if we were really and truly going out. It still wasn't official after all. Neither of us had said it yet. Okay, I had kind of said it to Casey when I was playacting, but that wasn't the same. I mean, Ethan hadn't said it to me yet. I guess technically we were just hanging out and making out and it was totally great, except... I ignored my brain. I wasn't saying anything first.

"Ready for the Pep Club?" I feigned my best Valley girl accent.

"Totally," Ethan mimicked my Valley girl accent back, as best as a guy could.

I grinned at him and we walked down the hallway toward the library, which was where the Pep Club was meeting. I was so focused on thinking about what might happen at this meeting and wondering if attending two meetings was definitely enough to legitimately and truthfully put this club on my college applications, that I almost didn't notice right away that Ethan had grabbed my hand. We were actually walking hand in hand toward the library, not to mention down the halls of the high school, on a school day. Even if it was after school and there weren't as many people around.

I forced myself not to look at Ethan or stop walking or give any sign that I had noticed. My stomach did an excited flip. It was really nice holding his hand. I felt myself start to smile. I looked down so Ethan wouldn't notice. I had to breathe. I was cool. I was totally cool. Oh no, now I wanted to smile even bigger.

We got to the library doors and Ethan pushed open the main door without letting go of my hand. I felt like we were a united front about to enter a war zone. It was sort of disconcerting, being that we were just entering the library and going to an after school club meeting.

The librarian directed us to a meeting room just off the main section of the library. It looked like a majority of the Pep Club members had turned up for the meeting. It was super packed. I noticed that Ariel was across the room, mostly because I heard Ariel shriek in surprise at seeing Ethan and I walk into the club meeting together. In her mind I knew we had just moved up a notch as a couple. Now, we were the couple that joined clubs together. If I thought about that, it did sound pretty serious, actually, almost as if we were boyfriend and girlfriend. Then again, I had to remind myself that we were only at the Pep Club meeting to see if we could discover any more murder clues and see what about the Pep Club presidency was potentially deadly.

Ethan and I sat down on the floor near the front

corner of the room. There were no seats left on chairs. The meeting was about to spill out into the main part of the library if any more people showed up. There was a general murmur of people talking and waiting for the meeting to start. Ethan and I held hands and listened. I tried to eavesdrop, but quickly got bored hearing people complain about teachers and classes or gush on about crushes. It almost seemed like people didn't want to talk about the murder on purpose. Maybe that was true, but I was pretty sure that's why the emergency Pep Club meeting had been called in the first place.

I glanced around the room and saw that I knew a few other people besides Ariel in Pep Club. There were a couple of random people from my classes, but nobody I really talked to, as well as Ariel's friends' Sarah and Megan. I also finally laid eyes on Sebastian Zane, Madison's date to the dance, who was trying to catch a nap in the corner. I'd have to try and talk to him before the meeting let out, even if he was probably in the clear.

It was a few minutes after three-thirty, which was when the meeting was supposed to start. That was when Mrs. Davis, the faculty member in charge of Pep Club, cleared her throat, cut straight through the crap, and said, "Welcome everyone. As you know tragedy has struck our club and we have lost two of our esteemed members in the last few days. Let us have a moment of silence and remember them."

As the group went silent, I looked around the room. Most people had their heads down and were looking at the floor. I glanced around for anyone who might feel the slightest bit guilty and be showing it in this moment. My eyes flicked to Sebastian, but he just looked startled at having been woken up. I moved on. Ariel's eyes met mine across the room. We both looked away quickly and the moment of silence was over.

Mrs. Davis continued, "What brings us here today for this emergency meeting is two fold. First, we need to elect a new Pep Club president. Then we need to talk about the football game on Saturday, make some posters, and show that school spirit is most important in times of tragedy. It binds us together as a school and the support will help us move on."

I felt like Mrs. Davis was being a little cheesy, although I agreed with the overall sentiment. Madison, and even Julia, deserved a tribute of school spirit. They did both love the Pep Club, even if they pretty much hated each other. Or, well, I knew it was technically more complicated than that.

"Since there is no successor, we need nominations from the junior or senior class for Pep Club President," Mrs. Davis said.

"Jenny Kendall!" a guy in the back yelled out.

I looked around to see who that might be, since I didn't know her and saw a girl with long black hair and skinny jeans wave to those who turned to look at her. Her friends were wildly pointing to her and cheering. I noticed a familiar looking girl with flaming red hair in a pixie cut, as one of the people cheering Jenny on. Wait a minute. I tried to place her, the girl with the pixie cut. I looked between Jenny and her friend. Then I remembered. I had seen them talking about Julia the other day. Now, I had one of their names. Interesting development.

"Sebastian Zane!" a girl called out and I saw Sebastian grin and throw up his hands in a Nixon-esque salute.

I glanced at Ethan, he looked back at me, eyebrows raised.

"Ariel Walker!" Sarah yelled.

I felt my brain freeze as I registered Ariel's glee at

being nominated for Pep Club President. Ariel looked around the room like she owned the place and just smiled. I knew from that smile that she was going to get her way and I was terrified.

Ten minutes later, I was proved right and Ariel was officially Pep Club president. She was practically glowing with pride the rest of the meeting. Why did Ariel of all people have to be the one to get elected president? I tried to not pay attention to her, so I wouldn't worry even more. Besides, Ethan and I had a poster to worry about and investigation work to do. Ethan and I grabbed our markers and blank poster board. Then I casually led Ethan over toward Sebastian, to position ourselves within talking distance of him.

Ethan and I looked at our poster board blankly. We needed to come up with something creative for cheering the football team on to victory. I know I didn't want to hold up or put up a poster that looked like a second grader drew it. I looked over toward Sebastian who was studying his blank poster board with some scrutiny. Maybe this was a way in.

"What are you going to draw?" I asked.

Sebastian looked up at me, "Probably just the mascot and the old standby: Go Palos Grizzlies!"

"That sounds simple," I said.

Sebastian nodded. We lapsed into silence. I was rapidly losing my chance to get information out of him.

"Hey, didn't you go to the dance with Madison Brown?" Ethan asked.

I looked at Ethan in relief. Somehow it sounded better coming from a popular guy to another popular guy.

"Yeah, I did," Sebastian said.

Ethan whispered, "And the cops don't consider you a suspect?"

Sebastian frowned, "Why would they? I'm not a girl, I was nowhere near the girl's bathroom, and I have friends who would back me up on that, since I was talking to them while Madison was gone."

It sounded like a pretty airtight alibi if Sebastian had a few people willing to vouch for him. Still, they might lie in order to protect a friend. It wasn't unheard of. I decided to play a morbid curiosity seeker. Hey, it fit my reputation.

"Who do you think would want to kill her?" I asked. "I mean, did she fight with anyone at the dance?"

"No, we were having a great time, actually," Sebastian said. "And, as to who might kill her...I have no idea. She was a great girl, although, we only went out a couple of times. Still, maybe someone like Julia Morgan would have had a reason. Then again she's dead too."

"Did you know her too?" I asked, trying to sound impressed by Sebastian knowing both of the dead girls.

"Some," Sebastian admitted, "Julia tried to hit on all the guys."

"I wonder who'd want both of them dead," Ethan said.

Sebastian laughed and said, "Jenny Kendall. She wanted to be Pep Club president just as much as either of them. Too bad Ariel took it from her today."

"But you were in the running too," I said.

"I'd do it if they elected me," Sebastian said, "But I don't really care. It's just a college transcript booster for me, but those girls were all at each other to be president like it was the holy grail of high school club status."

I looked over at Jenny Kendall. She was busy using glitter to decorate her poster. Could someone who used glitter be a murderer? She was working on the poster pretty ferociously, though. Ethan and I had barely started ours and Jenny was already snazzing hers up. Maybe she was venting her frustrations on losing the presidency into her art.

Sebastian must have seen me looking over at Jenny because he said, "She looks pretty innocent, though, right? Yeah, if it wasn't her, you might check out Madison's ex-boyfriend, Ray Newton. He and Julia had a thing too. Big love triangle."

Sebastian's friend, a big burly guy who totally didn't look like he'd belong in Pep Club, distracted him with a question about something normal, like a fantasy league of some kind. I wasn't into sports or fake sports or the like, so I quickly tuned out. I know. I was in Pep Club, which cheered sports teams on, but it was more about gawking at hot guys, getting a club on your college applications, and in this case, investigating some murders.

Ethan and I exchanged a glance. Another couple of names added to the suspect list and we still had to finish our Pep Club poster. We both looked down at it, since Sebastian had started talking to his friend.

"What do you want to draw?" Ethan asked, noticing my gaze.

"Anything to get us out of here," I said, looking down at the blank white poster board.

"Yeah," Ethan sighed.

I looked over toward Jenny Kendall. I wanted to talk to her too before Pep Club ended. I wouldn't have a more opportune moment. She wasn't in her spot, though. I looked around the room. Jenny wasn't in sight. She was already gone, poster done. She must have been upset about losing the presidency. Maybe she had stayed to keep up appearances and then booked out as soon as nobody was looking. I'd have to make it a point to catch up to her later.

Ethan and I walked out of Pep Club an hour later with marker stains on our hands from making posters for the game on Saturday. It was a lot of work, making a quality poster. At least, I hoped it hadn't looked like a kindergartner made it, since one of us was probably going to be holding it at the game, in front of the entire school. We were both silent. My mind for the last hour had been warring between how I might convince Ariel to denounce her Pep Club presidency and the idea that maybe Ariel could keep her new post because there was a different reason for the murders. I didn't want Ariel to take the chance. At this point, the odds weren't good.

"You okay?" Ethan asked as we walked to his car. He had driven to school in anticipation of going to the Pep Club meeting.

I shrugged, "Just worrying about Ariel. I know that's weird."

Ethan frowned, "It's not weird. You guys were best friends for forever."

I nodded, "Yeah. I guess I still care about her. You know, that she stays alive."

"You're only human," Ethan said, sarcastically, raising an eyebrow at me.

"Thanks," I punched him playfully on the arm.

He used the opportunity to try and tickle me. I ran. He chased me all the way to the car where he kissed me. Ariel became a distant memory for a few minutes.

We broke apart and I looked up at Ethan, "We have to figure out what's going on before Saturday."

"Why?" Ethan asked.

"I would bet anything that the next murder will take place then," I said simply.

"How do you know that?" Ethan asked. "The second murder happened on a random Tuesday."

"Yeah," I said, thinking, "Right before a Pep Club bake sale and the first one took place at the Homecoming Dance that the Pep Club helped decorate. Regardless, the game is sure a great place to kill someone and make a scene and I'm starting to think this killer gets off on ruining school events. They totally don't seem to have school spirit."

"Do you think that's the motive then?" Ethan asked. "Ruining school functions?"

"I think that's kind of a lame motive," I said, "I think it's more of a bonus. You know? Like they get off on the scandal and they're the only ones who know that they did it and got away with it...so far."

Ethan nodded, "That kind of makes sense. You know, as much as I hate to admit it, you kind of have a knack for this."

I felt a glow of pleasure at the compliment, "Thanks."

"So, any idea where to start?" Ethan asked.

Being that the list of potential suspects only seemed to be growing wasn't a good thing. I had lots of ideas, but no real solid leads. If we were going to figure things out by Saturday, we needed more connections between the dots.

My glow of pleasure disappeared, "None."

CHAPTER 14
POLICE CHATTING

It was Ethan's idea to visit Detective Dixon at the Palos Police Station. I wished I had some advance notice. I would have bought the Detective a reusable coffee mug. It was on my list. The Styrofoam cup thing he had going on was seriously bothering me. I didn't have too much time to think about it, though, because surprise, surprise we were ushered into his office way more quickly than that last time.

"What are you two doing here?" Detective Dixon asked gruffly.

I noticed that the Styrofoam cups in his office seemed to have multiplied. I really shouldn't have procrastinated on buying that travel mug. Actually, Detective Dixon's office really would have benefited from a cleaning service too, and of course, a recycling bin.

"We're here to talk about the murders of Madison Brown and Julia Morgan," I said.

Detective Dixon sighed, "Look, Kait and Ethan, like I've said before, leave this to the police. Enjoy high school."

"How can we? People are being murdered. And, we

helped you last time," I said, already regretting and second guessing Ethan's instinct at coming to the police station.

"We have some good information," Ethan said. "Maybe we could do a trade."

Detective Dixon's frown turned into a smirk, "The police don't work like that."

"We do have some leads," I said.

Detective Dixon looked at me, "Are you trying to end up in the hospital again?"

"No," I said. "Of course not."

"Are you sure? Do I need to put you on suicide watch?" Detective Dixon asked.

He was being sarcastic. I frowned at him, "No. "I'm just trying to find out what really happened to Madison and Julia."

Detective Dixon sighed, "Fine. What do you guys have?"

We told him our list of suspects and the reasons behind them from Noah Robertson to Sebastian Zane to Seth Wilcox to Jenny Kendall to Ray Newton. I secretly wondered how many more suspects might be in the woodwork.

"Oh, and Ariel Walker, despite having been in the bathroom with Madison right before she died, didn't do it," I said finally. "She told me all about it and I believe her."

I had to make that clear to the detective. I was pretty positive that Ariel had nothing to do with the murders of Madison and Julia. Well, ninety-nine percent sure and that was pretty sure. Plus, I didn't want the police spending time suspecting Ariel, when she might turn out to be the next victim.

"We talked to Ariel," Detective Dixon said, but didn't

say anything else.

A kernel of fear popped up in my stomach. Was Ariel a suspect then? Why didn't Detective Dixon say anything else? She couldn't be. Seriously, what if Ariel was the one in danger?

"Detective," I added, "Just a note, I mean, so you know - Ariel is the new Pep Club president. I mean, just in case she's in danger and all. And, like I said, she's not a murderer."

The Detective nodded. I didn't know if he'd help Ariel at all, but at least I had mentioned my fears to him. It was all I could do and at least it was something.

I was impressed, though, the whole time we talked, I noticed that Detective Dixon actually wrote our suspects down and seemed to genuinely listen, even about Ariel being in danger. He did write that down too. I could read it upside down on his notepad. It was a nice change of pace. Detective Dixon was taking us seriously this time. It looked like I had gotten some street cred from solving my last case.

"Anyone else a suspect?" Detective Dixon asked, pen poised.

Ethan and I looked at each other. The five names we had given the Detective were our lead suspects. Truthfully, the killer might not even be one of them. I wondered what sort of leads the police had and if there was anyone else we should add to the list. Then I noticed that the Detective had used the plural word for murders. So, the police were investigating Julia's death as a murder too. It was official, at least in police channels, even if nobody else knew that yet.

"No," Ethan said. "No other suspects."

Detective Dixon looked over the list, "Thanks. We'll take it from here."

"Can you give us anything?" I asked.

Detective Dixon shook his head, "I can't. Sorry. It's a police matter. Thank you for the help, though."

I nodded even though I was disappointed, "Yeah."

Detective Dixon hesitated, like he was going to say something.

"What?" I asked.

"I was just thinking that someday you might make a pretty good detective," Detective Dixon said.

I smiled at him. I almost said something about the Styrofoam cups and recycling, but I kept my mouth shut. Detective Dixon was paying me a compliment. It wasn't the time to criticize his impact on the planet.

Then the Detective continued on, "Someday when I'm retired of course and you've grown up. In the meantime, we've got it from here. Okay?"

I didn't say anything. I felt Ethan look at me. I wasn't promising anyone that I'd stop sleuthing. Detective Dixon didn't notice, though, he was busy hurrying us out of his office. Ethan and I walked out of the police station, hand in hand, toward his car.

"So, are you happy with how that turned out?" I asked. We hadn't gotten any real information to help us in our case, but from Detective Dixon's reaction to us, I felt like maybe we helped him with some insight into the background high school politics going on in this case. He had at least sort of listened to us this time around. Still, it would have been nice to get some clues for our investigation in return.

Ethan shrugged, "You?"

That was when we passed the police impound lot. I glanced over and something caught my eye. I spotted it from across the yard, actually. It was the car that had obviously been Julia's. It was a white Honda Civic, which was pretty boring and it would not have stood out at all, except that the front hood was up and written inside the front hood, I could just make out the words: Pep Club slut.

CHAPTER 15
ZEALOUS SLEUTHING

It was finally Friday. It had been an excruciatingly long week. From Madison's murder to Julia's to rejoining Pep Club to worrying for Ariel, I had been busy. That wasn't including things like homework and my job at the video store or time spent making out with Ethan.

I had spent the night before tossing and turning, wondering if the Pep Club really was the basis for the murders. Was anti-school spirit really that strong of a motivator for someone to kill innocent girls?

I was tired and had to rush to get ready for school. I forgot to put on my make-up and only remembered when I was almost at the bus stop. I couldn't go back home and get it because I was already running late. Then, I barely caught my bus on time - as in, I had to run after it. Luckily, the bus driver saw me and stopped to pick me up. It was going to be one of those days.

Madison's funeral was after school. Ethan and I decided to attend it together. I'd have time to go home and change this time, since we were going to go a couple of hours after school ended. Thank goodness, since I at least, wanted to put on some make-up for that.

I saw Ariel hanging Pep Club posters inviting everyone

to the game on Saturday, just as I walked in the school doors. It freaked me out a little and hit home that I better move forward in the murder investigation. I saw Ariel notice me as I walked by too, but she pretended not to see me. Typical. I ignored her too and hurried to my locker.

As muddled as my brain felt from the exhausting week and it being way too early in the morning, I knew I had to be on my toes. I needed to investigate some of the leads Ethan and I had. It was Friday and we were running out of time until Saturday. I was still sure that Saturday was the D-day for the next murder and I was really afraid that Ariel was the next one in danger of being killed.

I realized that I should have asked Ariel about Ray Newton, Madison and Julia's ex, but only after I was on my way to first period. Maybe Madison had talked about Ray to her friends. I was really out of it tired. I needed a pop or one of those super duper energy boosting drinks with ginseng or whatever. If I got a chance to, I made a mental note to ask Ariel about Ray later. I had looked Ray up in the yearbook and he was on my list of people to talk to if I could find him. Ray hadn't looked like the kind of guy who could tear two best friends apart by dating each of them, but maybe he was really charming and conned you into falling for him. Ray Newton just wasn't off the page hot.

I saw Jenny Kendall at her locker after second period. I remembered where it was after seeing her and her friend talking the other day and I had purposely changed my route to class to try and talk to her. I was done with worrying if I'd look like a nutcase. Ariel's life might be on the line. I was really worried.

"So, are you mad that you weren't elected Pep Club president?" I asked, as I walked up to Jenny.

Jenny looked up at me in surprise. I could see that she was trying to place how I knew her and how I meant my question to see how she should answer it. That was high school.

"I'm in Pep Club," I said, clarifying for her. I thought attending two meetings definitely meant I was in the club and could put it on my college applications without worrying about lying.

"Well, I mean, I'm disappointed," Jenny offered, "But Ariel will make a good president. Are you with the school newspaper too or something?"

"No," I said, "Just curious. I heard you really wanted to be president even when Madison and Julia were elected."

Jenny shrugged, "I did. I still do, but there's nothing I can do about it. The club voted."

"Well, if Ariel were to disappear..." I started.

Jenny's eyebrows shot up, "Hey, I wouldn't kill anyone for the job. It's a stupid club. You're weird."

Then Jenny shut her locker and walked away from me. I hadn't really thought that she'd admit to killing Madison or Julia. It was worth asking, though. She had seemed honest enough. I hadn't gotten a vibe from her or anything, at least. That counted for something. Jenny was at the bottom of my suspect list for now. I couldn't take her off, just because the Pep Club presidency was still a to-die-for job, until I found another motive for the murders. Besides, it was completely possible that Jenny was a really good actress. Still, I moved her to the bottom of the list.

I walked to class wondering if I was overlooking anything. There were five suspects and some seemed guiltier than others, but nobody was standing out to me, like they had the last time. That worried me. I felt overwhelmed and I was afraid that Ariel's time was running out. Should I be doing more? Like, trying to dig up some more names or digging deeper into the ones I already had? There was no time! I had to calm down. I could do this. Ethan and I would save Ariel in time and figure out who was committing the murders.

In Chemistry class, I was floored to find Kyle and Suzie blatantly making out at my lab table. That was kind of surprising in that they were normally so awkward and quiet, but love obviously was winning out over that. Still, I wasn't quite sure what to do. I definitely had third wheel feelings and it was all really awkward. What did one do in these situations? How was I going to get to my chair without knocking into them? Plus, I knew the teacher would freak out on them if they were caught, even though at the moment, I knew they could care less.

"Ahem," I said loudly.

Kyle and Suzie jumped apart with a giggle.

"Sorry," Kyle said.

Suzie's cheeks were pink.

"No, I'm sorry to interrupt," I said. "I just figured that it would be better if it was me than the teacher."

"True," Kyle said.

"How's the investigation going?" Suzie asked.

"It's going okay," I said and then gave them the details. I was beyond caring if they knew I was teen sleuthing. They had already guessed it anyway.

"But what about Madison's other friends? Or Julia's? Or, someone else on the inside of the Pep Club? Or a faculty member?" Kyle said, throwing out more suspects.

I frowned at him, "Kyle, you're not helping."

That being said, I made a mental note to make a list of secondary suspects after I ran through the short list. I had to skip lunch with Ethan to do a makeup quiz for math. I hoped I passed it. I really had been spending way too much time murder investigating and not enough time catching up on homework and classes. I needed a work life balance. And, an Ethan balance somewhere in there too. I missed having lunch with him.

I looked for Ray Newton, throughout the day, but our paths never crossed. I had to find out more about him. Maybe he'd be at Madison's funeral.

The weird kid Logan Collins' mentioned, Seth Wilcox, was actually in my last period class. He was the typical outcast - longish black hair that curled about his neck, dark t-shirt, ripped jeans. We had never spoken just because I never talked to anyone, although I had always gotten the idea that Seth was pretty antisocial too. I had never gotten the impression that he was dangerous or malicious, though, just quiet and wary of the rest of the high school students. I could understand that. I was wary and unsure of them, myself.

"Hey," I said, sitting down next to Seth. There was no seating chart for this class, so I had a good four minutes to talk to Seth before the bell rang without worrying that I was sitting in someone else's seat.

Seth looked up at me with distrust, "What do you want?"

It felt like my standard, cautious response. I wondered if Seth had an Ariel sort of person in his life too that made him act like this.

"I wanted to talk to you about Madison Brown and Julia Morgan," I said.

Seth's eyebrows shot up at hearing the murdered girls' names, "Why is that?"

"I'm investigating their deaths," I said.

"But you're not a cop," Seth said.

"No," I said. "I just want to find out what happened to

them. I think it's sad and whoever did it deserves to be caught."

"I heard a rumor that you crash funerals," Seth said.

"That's true," I said.

"And, that you're dating Ethan Ripley?" Seth asked, eyebrows raised.

"Well," I said, unsure. "We're hanging out."

Seth nodded knowingly, but I noticed his eyes narrow for a moment as he took in the fact that I was dating a popular guy. He definitely had trust issues with the popular crowd, "Okay. And, now you're telling me you're a female sleuth?"

"Yes," I said.

"So, why do you think I know something about Julia Morgan and Madison Brown's deaths?" Seth asked.

I was caught. I decided to tell the truth, "Logan Collins said that you were harassing Madison and hated Pep Club."

Seth continued to nod, thoughtfully, "He did?"

"Yes," I said, watching Seth curiously.

Seth said nothing. He was obviously thinking something over. I suddenly got the distinct impression that this guy was actually really, really smart. He didn't do or say anything - it was just the way he was thinking in front of me. I could have been totally wrong, of course, but I didn't think so. Seth was totally antisocial and didn't trust anyone, but I was pretty sure that he had a smart brain on his shoulders. I wondered if Seth got good grades or didn't care. It could go either way.

"Let me tell you about Logan Collins. He's a total dick," Seth said.

This time my eyebrows shot up, "You want to tell me why?"

"Well, he's popular," Seth said.

"Okay. What else?" I asked.

"He used to be one of my best friends in junior high and then he ditched me," Seth said.

Wow, how many broken friendships was I going to be investigating during this case? I had my own to worry about and mull over.

"What did he ditch you for?" I asked.

"Madison Brown and Julia Morgan," Seth said.

"Oh, I'm sorry," I said.

It gave Seth a huge reason for murder, although it was about four to seven years late. Still, it was something to consider. Ariel and mine's friendship had fallen apart over a year ago and it still felt pretty fresh.

"I'm not," Seth said, "We weren't meant to be friends forever."

I didn't quite believe Seth. I heard the slight anger in his voice when he talked about Logan. He had obviously cooled down in the years since his and Logan's friendship implosion, but even I knew, it wasn't true that you didn't feel anything at the breakup of a friendship, especially if you were the one being ditched for someone better and more cool.

"So, do you want to say anything to Logan's accusation that you were harassing Madison?" I asked.

Seth shrugged, "Just that it's not true, but I know you won't believe me."

"Why not?" I asked.

"Because Logan's hotter and more popular and thus, his words have more weight," Seth said.

It was true, funny enough. I wondered who people would believe if Ariel and I were in a similar situation. Everyone would probably believe her, actually, although it would definitely be more likely that I was telling the truth. I really did know where Seth was coming from. He was in big trouble if Logan really decided to point fingers to say, the police. Logan had a way of bewitching people. Seth just had a way of making them mad at him. Yeah, Seth was in definite trouble if push came to shove. I had gotten what I came for, though, a general impression of him. No murderer was going to admit to anything. Impressions were what you had to go on.

"Thanks," I said. "I appreciate you talking to me."

"Whatever," Seth said and put his head on his hands and went to sleep.

I pulled out my investigation notebook as I heard Seth start snoring. He sure fell asleep fast. I wrote down some notes until the bell rang.

CHAPTER 16
FUNERAL CRASHING

When I got home, I changed into my best funeral clothes, taking extra care on my hair and makeup. We may have been going to a funeral, but Ethan and I were going as a couple and the whole school was going to show up to it. As much as I had crashed funerals, I had never been to the funeral of someone from my school. Nobody I knew like that had ever died and it was making me feel a little spooked. It made it feel like it could happen to me. I tried to distance myself from it. Death was a part of life. One had to accept that. It was just the fact that she was my age that really bothered me. Well, that and that I had been at the Homecoming Dance too.

I felt like crying and I didn't even really know Madison. I took a deep breath and looked at my watch. Ethan was going to arrive at any moment. I couldn't have running mascara and be a wreck when he showed up. I dabbed at my eyes with a tissue. My cell phone rang. Ethan was outside.

I walked out to Ethan's car and got in. Our eyes met and I could see that he was just as affected by the idea of going to Madison's funeral as I was. Ethan smiled at me.

"You too, huh?" Ethan said.

"Yeah," I forced myself to smile back at him.

"How are we going to look for a murderer at this thing?" Ethan asked, pulling out of the driveway and onto the street. "I'm not sure I'm going to be able to sit through it."

"I know what you mean," I said, leaning back into the passenger seat, wishing I could take a long nap instead of going to the funeral, "This is going to take a lot out of me. We just have to remember that we're doing this so we don't have any more high school funerals to go to."

Ethan nodded. I declined mentioning that Julia's funeral was next week. We already had a second funeral to attend. It made it even more imperative that we catch the killer. Although the quick flash in my head of attending Ariel's funeral was really all the incentive I needed to steel myself to the idea of carrying on an investigation at Madison's funeral even when I felt like I should spend it in mourning.

We drove up to the Worth Hills Funeral Home. The last time I was there Ethan and I were investigating his half sister's murder. Ethan didn't say anything about that, though, as he pulled into the parking spot. I wondered if Ethan was thinking about his half sister Liz too. I hoped he was doing okay with it all. Since we had solver her murder, Ethan hadn't talked much about her. I could understand that, though. I just hoped he knew he could talk to me.

I couldn't help thinking how far we had come since that day, the time we were last at Worth Hills Funeral Home. That time we had feigned being boyfriend and girlfriend and now we almost were. It had in no way been defined yet, of course, but since then we had gone to a dance together, made out in a parked car, and held hands walking down a school hallway. We had to be pretty close to being the real deal.

Ethan held out his hand to me. I took it. I felt safe and secure holding his hand. At least, I did, right up until we walked through the front doors of the funeral home.

"You!" A man walking out of the funeral home office said.

I looked around for the person he was talking to, but then realized he was staring at me. He was tall and thin with very little brownish black hair left on his head and he was dressed in funeral suit black. I didn't know him, except for maybe seeing him around at the funerals because he managed or owned the place or something.

While I was trying to place him, he walked up to us and said, "I need to ask you to leave."

I was confused, "Why?"

"You crash funerals," the man said. "I've seen you here attending them. You need to leave."

I frowned at him, "I know the girl who died. I was in Pep Club with her."

The man looked at me like I was lying, "Please leave."

I wasn't sure what the rule to funeral crashing was when the Funeral Home Director found you out. Maybe it was wear a disguise or just simply never go to that funeral home again. I wondered how he had found me out, though. I had never actually gotten caught by a guest and gotten in trouble, well, almost, once, but I ran away and it was at a different funeral home. I didn't count that time with Ariel and Leonora. That was different. And, well, Ethan caught me too, but I know that he didn't snitch on me.

Then again, the whole school was at this funeral and I did have a weird graveyard girl, funeral crashing reputation. Someone probably just thought it would be funny to get me kicked out of Madison's funeral. Ariel's name flashed through my brain, but I didn't think she was a tattler. She was much more of a gossip.

I looked sideways at Ethan to see how he was taking this latest development. I wasn't sure what to do. I definitely didn't want to cause a scene at a funeral, especially one that probably most of my high school was going to be attending. Yet, it was really important that I be at this funeral. How did we get out of this?

Wow, I hadn't thought of it, but Madison's funeral was really going to be a blending of my two worlds. That was surreal. I was curious to walk further into the funeral home, but the Funeral Director was still blocking my way.

"I do know Madison Brown," I said again. "I can show you my school ID and prove that I went to school with her."

The Funeral Director shook his head, "Please leave before I call the police."

"The police are here," A voice said from behind us.

Ethan and I turned to look and found ourselves face to face with Detective Dixon. Uh-oh. The last time we had seen him at a funeral, we had to make a run for it. This was not going to be good, even if he had paid me a compliment a couple of days ago.

"Detective Dixon, you have to listen to us, we are seriously here to mourn Madison Brown," I said, rambling.

"I know," Detective Dixon said, looking between Ethan and me, "And, I expect that's all you'll be doing. Right?"

"Yes, sir," Ethan said.

I nodded my agreement. It was a lie. I mean, I'd keep it on the down low and everything, but I couldn't promise not to pay attention and try to discover more clues if the opportunity arose. Other people were going to be talking about the murder. It's not like I couldn't partake. It was a free country. Still, Detective Dixon didn't need to know that and Ethan and I were really there to mourn Madison. I was genuinely sad to be at her funeral.

The Funeral Director was looking at Detective Dixon like he'd grown horns and joined a cult. I didn't blame him. It wasn't often a policeman took the side of some meddling teenagers.

The Funeral Director frowned at us, "Just be sure you do."

Yeah, I wasn't going to be hitting up this funeral home anytime soon unless I dyed my hair and wore a disguise. I hadn't even done anything wrong by attending those other funerals. I mean, I hadn't known the deceased, but it wasn't like I'd wreaked havoc on the funeral or wake or anything. I'd have to start being more careful. Maybe disguises were a good idea, actually. It might be fun to play a different part every time.

Ethan took my hand and brought me out of my thoughts as he said, "We're going to go into the viewing room now."

Ethan led me away from Detective Dixon and the Funeral Director, who turned to look at each other. I was sure they were going to have a conversation that I didn't want to hear. I was sure it was all about me.

"That was close," I said as we walked down the hallway to the viewing room.

The walk was a little surreal being that the hallway was littered with people from high school. It was like walking down a high school corridor, but in a funeral home. Everyone was staring you down, sizing you up, and yet, half of them had tissues and were dabbing their eyes. Overall, it was a very strange moment for me.

"You need to be more careful," Ethan warned, bringing me out of my thoughts.

"I know," I said. "I'm thinking costumes and disguises."

Ethan looked at me, amused, "Really?"

"Yeah," I shrugged, "Really. I mean, it's a free country and I'm not disturbing anything. I just need to make sure I don't get caught and arrested or anything, though. My dad would kill me."

Ethan shook his head, "I can't believe I'm dating a girl who likes funerals so much that she's willing to invent disguises."

I knew it was a weird trait on my part, so Ethan's statement didn't bother me. He was getting used to it. What was bothering me more was that Ethan had said the word dating. I focused on that word in the sentence. What did it mean? Was that the telltale sign that we were now boyfriend and girlfriend? Or, did dating in this connotation just mean hanging out? It really shouldn't have been this confusing. It was driving me nuts trying to figure this out. Maybe I could help the answer along...

I had to reply to Ethan's statement with something witty and light and about dating, "Well, at least you know that dating a funeral crasher won't be boring."

I looked at Ethan to see if he would flinch at the word dating. He didn't. So, why didn't he say the word girlfriend? It would really help my brain out.

"It's definitely not boring," Ethan grinned and I smiled back at him. He was so cute.

Then Ethan's smile faded and he squeezed my hand. We were entering the viewing room for Madison Brown and the air was heavy with mourning. I felt my smile die too and my heart went out to Madison and her family.

CHAPTER 17
EULOGY GIVING

Madison Brown was more popular for having died than she ever would have been in high school, including her time as Pep Club president. She had a little over three hundred friends on Facebook and the viewing room was packed. Every one of those friends was there, plus more. This was only the start of the night. People would come in and out all night. Girls were crying. I sort of wondered if some of them even knew Madison or were putting on a show for their friends. Was it heartless of me to think that? I didn't think so. If you've ever been a girl in high school, you know that sometimes people just play a part. There sure were a lot of girls pressing tissues to their teary eyes and looking up into handsome boy's eyes to see the effect. And, hey, Ethan and I officially connected at a funeral, so I won't say it doesn't work, but I didn't go to that funeral trying to pick up guys. Just saying.

Looking around the room, I started to think that maybe our promise to Detective Dixon would end up being true. There were so many people at the funeral that it would be hard to investigate it. Somehow I didn't think the murderer was going to stand up at the front of the room and give a eulogy or anything. What would they start with? Something like - You're all here today because of me?

Ethan and I walked up to the casket. I hadn't seen Madison since that long ago day at the school year's first Pep Club meeting, but I was amazed at how much she looked like she was sleeping. I felt a wave of sadness pass through me. We had to move on, but I just wanted to stay there and look at her for a little longer. I felt Ethan pull my hand. I took one last look and we walked toward the back of the room and blended in with the other high school students that were milling around.

It really felt like the whole school had shown up for the funeral. It was completely possible that Madison's murderer was present, pretending to mourn her too. Ethan and I were surrounded by people from school. Some of them were seniors and looked familiar, but I didn't know them. We waded our way into the crowd of people, slowly, listening to conversations as we passed. Some people were whispering about the murder, afraid to talk too loudly in case someone who really knew Madison got upset about it. Other people were truly upset and crying, with friends consoling them. And other people weren't talking about Madison at all, but about high school stuff like: "Oh my gosh. Jason Gregory is so cute. Do you think he'll talk to me?" I sort of wanted to listen in on that one because it made me wonder who Jason was and if he would talk to the girl in question, but Ethan kept moving forward. I followed him. We were on a mission. We had more important conversations to eavesdrop on.

I stopped short as a super cute little girl with short brown curly hair ran in front of me, all dressed in black. I almost stepped on her. Then she turned to look at me and my breath caught. She was smiling and she looked so much like a little version of Madison that it scared me for a moment. This little girl had her same catchy grin. She had to be Madison's little sister, Lana. The obituary had mentioned her. I guessed her to be about three or four. She was positively adorable. Poor kid. I didn't have any siblings, but no child should have to deal with their big sister dying. I thought of Ethan's little sister, Lilly. We hadn't officially met yet because I hadn't been to Ethan's house to meet anyone officially, but Lilly had lost a sibling at a young age too. She and Lana had something really sad in common. Still, kids were resilient. I hoped Lana would be okay.

I saw that Lana was chasing a little boy and playing. She had darted in front of me, to catch him in a game of tag. I was sure that there had been a lot of tears shed for her sister, but Lana had moved on and was able to play. Tonight, when Lana got home, I was sure there would be more tears as Lana realized that her sister wasn't coming home from the funeral. I didn't beget Lana playing. She was dealing with death in her own way, as a kid. I was glad that kids had that resiliency. It really protected them. I knew her sister's death would affect Lana all of her life, but at least for now she could still play.

"You're it!" Lana yelled after tagging the little boy.

Everyone near Lana turned to look at her, scolding in their eyes, but her parents were at the front mourning their daughter. Nobody dared say anything. You could see who she was if you knew Madison or even if you had just looked in the coffin. I wanted little Lana to play on. I hoped nobody would say anything. The little boy turned and ran after Lana and they ran out of the room, continuing their game of tag.

"I'm hungry," I whispered to Ethan. Besides, I was

starting to feel really sad about Madison and her little sister.

"Okay," Ethan said. "Let's go get some cookies."

Ethan and I went into the kitchen to see if there were any snacks. Nine times out of ten, people brought something for guests to munch on. I hadn't eaten anything after getting home from school because I had to get ready and put on makeup, so I was sort of starving. Thank goodness someone had brought a ton of cookies. The last funeral Ethan and I had been to had cookies too, but sometimes there wasn't anything to eat. That happened too. This time there was a smorgasbord - besides the cookies there were tons of chips, veggies and dip, and cheese and crackers too. Someone had gone all out at the grocery store in the snacks section. They expected the high school kids to eat, obviously.

I reached for a chocolate chip cookie and bumped into someone. It was Noah Robertson, of course.

"Are you serious?" Noah looked down at me and said.

I looked at him with the exact same incredulous expression that he had on his face, "I'm sorry. I didn't do it on purpose. I just wanted a cookie."

Noah frowned at me, grabbed five cookies and limped away. I felt annoyed and then puzzled. His cast was on the wrong foot. Or had I remembered it wrong? I stared at him until he disappeared. Was Noah lying about his foot? Maybe I was mistaken. I thought back to running into him earlier in the week. Which foot had the cast been on? Or was I just looking for something, anything, to catch the killer? Maybe my brain was just starting to make stuff up. Still...

"What was that about?" Ethan asked from behind me.

"You don't want to know," I shook my head and scooped up a few chocolate chip cookies, resolving to keep an eye on Noah's feet.

Ethan and I went into the lounge with our snacks. I wondered if I was going to get a stomachache from the cookies and coffee I was having for my after school lunch slash dinner. Ethan was eating the same linner, except that he had a couple more peanut butter cookies than I did. Those looked good, actually, but I stopped myself from going to get more. Maybe we could stop and get some fast food on our way home.

There were a lot of people in the lounge and it was proving to be a good location for people watching. I caught a glimpse of Ariel, but then she was gone into the viewing room.

For a while I watched Sebastian Zane talking to some of his friends in a corner, like he was holding court. He and Jenny Kendall were vying for the most people talking to them. I recognized a lot of people in both of their groups from the Pep Club meeting. I wondered if they were still campaigning for Pep Club president. Or, maybe they were forming Anti-Ariel sects of the club. I just couldn't believe that they were doing it at Madison Brown's funeral. Maybe they were hoping for some sort of posthumous support from Madison, like a seal of approval from the casket. I wondered what they had planned for Julia's funeral.

"Hey, you two," Logan Collins said, sitting down beside us.

This was weird. I was sitting between two of the hottest guys at my school - one from the senior class and one from the junior class - at a funeral. I felt like I had entered *The Twilight Zone*. I was almost waiting for the music from the old TV show to start playing in the funeral home. Why was Logan sitting with us? Sure, Ethan was popular, but I wasn't and Ethan and I were both juniors, while Logan was a senior and...

"Have you found any more clues in Madison and Julia's deaths?" Logan asked.

Ethan and I looked at each other. This was the first time anyone outside of our group seemed to genuinely want to hear about our investigation. It was actually kind of cool, like we were really on the case! I didn't count Julia, of course, because that whole conversation was weird and who knew what her ulterior motives were. I would probably never get a chance to understand her either, since she was dead and all.

I tried not to stare at Logan and concentrated on speaking. I was nonchalant, not sure what I should give away just in case Logan was a gossiper, "Same old, same old. You don't by any chance know Ray Newton, do you?"

I actually felt a little like Detective Dixon, being so vague. Funny. I would not under any circumstances, though, start using Styrofoam cups.

Logan frowned, "He's a senior...right?"

"Yeah," I said. "Supposedly he dated both Madison and Julia."

"I don't really know him," Logan said.

"It was worth a shot," I said.

I wondered if Ray would show up at the funeral. I still wanted to talk to Ariel about him. Regardless, he was the only suspect I hadn't actually spoken to yet.

"Hey, guys," Suzie said, walking up, holding Kyle's hand.

Kyle looked wearily at Logan, but didn't say anything. Suzie must have reassured Kyle that despite Logan's hotness, he was no match for Kyle's brains. Or, well, that was the one compliment I could think of, at least, that was true.

Then Kyle and Suzie were suddenly sitting with us and Ethan's friends Dave and Mike came over and just like at the Homecoming Dance, I felt like we were forming a weird clique of popular/unpopular that was totally against all the rules of high school. Plus we were at a funeral. Silence descended over everyone. It was awkward. Thank goodness the memorial service was going to begin within the hour so we wouldn't have to deal with the weirdness for very long. Maybe Ethan and I could go for more cookies.

It was almost seven o'clock when the service began. Ethan and I managed to garner a seat in the packed room, which was lucky. I had feigned having to go to the bathroom and we had escaped the others after ten minutes of awkward conversation. My feet were killing me. We had already been at the funeral a long time and I was wearing heels, so I was glad for the seat. There were more people standing outside. I saw Detective Dixon near the back, trying to blend into the masse of high school students who were in attendance. They easily outnumbered the amount of relatives. Everyone who was anyone was at this funeral. I saw Ariel standing along another wall with Troy. It was sweet of him to come with her.

A priest said some religious words, the room shrouded in silence. Then the eulogies began. It was the most heartbreaking, touching, amazing part of the wake or funeral for me. I loved hearing people's memories. It was the one thing that kept the dead, alive, eternally.

When my mom died, a bunch of people gave eulogies. I was in super depressed mode and I didn't want to write one for her or speak in front of everyone. It was cool to hear what everyone else had to say, though, to see what they thought about my mom. I really appreciated the memories I didn't have of her told to me. Still, I wish I had spoken. There was a lot I had to say about my mom. The problem was that now, when I wanted to say them and talk about my memories, there was usually nobody around with whom to share the memories. The people who really knew my mom had been at the funeral and I didn't see them all that often. It would have been nice to share my memories with them.

Madison's dad was the first one to speak. He barely got through a minute talking about what a wonderful girl Madison had grown up to be and how he had been so very proud of her. He opened up the floor to anyone who wanted to speak about Madison and got away from the podium before he burst into tears. My heart almost broke watching him speak about his daughter. There wasn't a dry eye in the room.

Next was Madison's little sister, Lana. A relative led her up to the podium and stood next to her. You could tell that she was a little scared to be facing all of the people that had come to her big sister's funeral, but she was determined.

"I loved my sister a lot. I'll miss her times a billion," Lana said quickly, but with such emphasis, my heart twisted at her words.

Then I noticed that Lana had something in her hand, a piece of paper. It looked like a hand drawn card, although I couldn't see what she had drawn clearly. Lana walked from the podium to the casket and placed the card in it, next to her sister. Then she ran back to her parents and buried her face in her mom's shirt.

It was that simple. All those girls who were feigning tears earlier in the night, were full on bawling now. This time, they really meant it. I felt a tear of my own slide down my face. I wiped it away with my hand. I caught

Ethan glancing at me. He took my hand in his.

I didn't even hear the next eulogy. Madison's uncle spoke about his niece, but I spent the few minutes, trying to recompose myself, so that I wouldn't burst into tears. I concentrated on holding Ethan's hand and breathing. I felt better. Madison's uncle left the podium.

The spot was vacant for only a second when, to my surprise, Ariel walked up to the podium and looked out over the crowd dramatically, "I felt like I should say something as the new Pep Club president. Madison loved Pep Club and I only hope I can do as good of a job as Madison did. She was an amazing president."

Ariel looked like she was meant for standing at a podium, giving a speech, and I think she knew it. I almost felt like I was watching her on the big screen, in a movie. Ariel could be so confident and self-assured. I really admired that about her and despite the Pep Club campaign I knew she was waging, I knew Ariel really cared about Madison.

"Madison was also a good friend," Ariel said as if on cue and then to my shock, Ariel started faltering in her speech, with the weight of her words, "I actually only met Madison this year, but we really connected. I wish I had known her sooner. It's hard to believe that she's gone. We just went Homecoming Dress shopping and I know she was really excited about the dance and her date with Sebastian. It's just so weird. I mean, we won't get to talk about the dance and how it went or well, anything... She was just really cool."

Ariel got off the stage and burst into tears. Wow. Ariel had feelings. I wondered what she'd say if I ever died and if she'd cry. Ariel ran into Troy's arms. I watched him enfold her in his embrace. It struck me that they seemed to be a real couple now too. They looked great together.

Troy stroked Ariel's hair. I hoped he really cared about her. I hoped she really cared about him. I did really think he was a cool guy. Wow, everyone was pairing up and becoming boyfriend/girlfriend. I felt Ethan hand's in mine. Maybe even us.

That was when I noticed the guy standing next to them. It was Ray Newton. He had made an appearance, finally! After the speeches, Ethan and I needed to go over and talk to him. I studied him. Ray was a little cuter in person than in his yearbook photo. Still, he was kind of geeky and I wouldn't have pegged him for the ladies man type. Suddenly, my brain was distracted by the new voice at the podium and I looked away from Ray.

Logan had gone up to speak, "Hey. I knew Madison in junior high...."

Now, Logan was a ladies man. The room grew quiet at his hotness. Logan was silent in return. The crowd gazed at him, adoringly.

Logan drew a deep breath and continued, "There were a bunch of us who used to be really good friends, actually, and then we kind of drifted apart in high school. I feel sad about that. That we weren't as good of friends when Madison died."

Logan looked out at the crowd, silent again. Then he went on as if there was something more he had to say, "The Madison I remember was always laughing. We had a lot of fun together riding bikes - me, Madison, and Julia. The three burritos we used to call ourselves. I thought that was the right word for friends. Madison and Julia teased me about it. Amigos, they said. It became our inside joke."

Logan smiled at the thought. The room smiled with him. Then he abruptly left the podium, as if he couldn't take the memories. Logan disappeared into the crowd of students. I still couldn't get over the fact that Suzie Whitsett, shy quiet girl, knew Logan. That was still stupefying to me. It was so weird.

A few people I didn't know walked up to the podium. They were in Madison's classes or knew her from Pep Club and they all said the same thing - she was awesome and gone too soon. There were a few relatives who made brief speeches too. I filed all of their names away, just in case. My heart felt heavy.

Then Sebastian swaggered up to the stage and stood in front of the podium like he owned the place and I refocused, "I just wanted to say, Madison was a beautiful girl. Peace."

That was all Sebastian said and then he got offstage, giving the Nixon salute again. He wasn't trying to campaign, was he? Ariel had been doing a little of her own campaigning, but at least she said something real. Sebastian's words were completely fake, even if they were so high school. I heard some snickers. Sebastian and his friends should be the ones getting thrown out of the funeral.

I was annoyed to see then that Jenny took Sebastian's lead and was the next person up to the podium, "Madison was a wonderful Pep Club president. She was really and truly inspiring to all of us. She was a model of school spirit that I know I will try and emulate. We miss you Madison. Go Palos Grizzlies!"

Jenny walked away from the podium and it was obvious from the murmurs that she had garnered some votes for her sect by speaking. Politics was such a dirty business and we were only in high school. Need I mention that all of this was happening at a funeral? Over a club? I was really disturbed. The podium was for people who cared about the deceased. Not people trying to overthrow a club president so they could be president. I wanted to do something about it before someone else got up to speak.

I let go of Ethan's hand and made my way toward the podium. What was I doing? I didn't really know Madison and yet I felt a sudden urge to say something about her. Maybe it was because of the high school crap that was airing itself out at the podium, when it should have been left at the high school. Maybe it was because little Lana's speech had inspired me. Maybe it was because I hadn't said anything at my mom's funeral or any other funeral I had been to, for that matter. Right now though, I did have something to say.

I walked up to the podium and felt the eyes of the entire high school student body on me. I should have been nervous. I should have been trying to figure out what to say. I felt my knees start to shake uncontrollably, then my hands.

I had to speak, "I didn't really know Madison Brown all that well. I admit it, but I still felt moved to say something about her. From everyone's eulogies and from the gossip I've heard at school and from members of the Pep Club, I've only heard that Madison was a supremely cool girl. You all know that. That's why you're all here or why you should be here, at least. From what I know about Madison, most of all, she loved the Pep Club. She was all about school spirit and cheering on our high school's sports teams. She helped decorate the Homecoming Dance for all of you. She wanted to make high school an amazing experience, not only for herself, but for everyone standing in this room. I know that everyone is really sad about losing her, but I think we owe it to Madison Brown to make Saturday's football game against the Riverside Raiders so full of school spirit that winning or losing doesn't matter - it's about seizing the day, enjoying a simple football game, and cheering your heart out. I think we owe it to Madison to have a great time and remember that she would want us to keep cheering, keep laughing, and keep a little pep in our step. Let's have some pep club cheer for Madison."

I actually felt good talking at the podium. I could tell that my audience was connecting with what I said. That was when a kid all in black and wearing a ski mask decided to run into the room and throw black goo all over me. I didn't even know what happened. All of a sudden I was covered in the stuff. I wondered if *Carrie* felt like this at the prom. I don't know what I would have done if it was pig's blood. Goo was gross enough. Was I going to be able to get this stuff off?

Of course this would happen to me. This sort of thing only happened to me. How could they have known I'd speak, though, if I didn't know I was going to speak? Maybe it wasn't meant for me. Then who was it meant for?

There was pandemonium. People were freaking out. I wasn't dead, but I must have looked scary. Suddenly Ethan was standing in front of me, not knowing what to do because I was covered in goo.

"I'm fine," I said, although I think I was in shock.

I wasn't hurt, though. That was the truth. What had happened to the offender? I saw a big crowd in the hallway. I wondered if Detective Dixon had caught the guy.

"Kait," Ethan said again.

He had been trying to get my attention while I was distracted by the commotion in the hallway. I looked at him. He saw that I was finally paying attention.

"Let me get you out of here," Ethan said. "We need to

clean you off."

I nodded and walked out of the funeral home with Ethan. I was still in shock. My brain felt numb. I didn't want to touch anything in case I ruined it, so I just carefully followed him, trying not to move too much.

The police showed up fast, followed by an ambulance. Ethan and I were just about at his car when we were flagged down by a policeman.

"Hey, wait. I need a statement from you," The policeman said.

Ethan and I stopped to look at him. He was a young policeman with slightly too long for a cop, brown hair. It made him look almost our age, if he wasn't wearing a police uniform. In fact, he couldn't have been that much older than us. His name tag said Quincy.

"I just want to go home," I said.

"We need a statement," Officer Quincy said again. "And, you should get checked out by the paramedics."

"I'm okay," I said, even though I felt myself shaking. "I mean, I'm not hurt. I don't need to see the paramedics. It's just goo."

"Are you sure?" Officer Quincy peered down at me. He had brown eyes.

I knew I was covered in goo and looked terrible, but I was pretty sure I was not actually injured. I was mortified. I was freaked out, but I was not hurt.

"I'm sure," I said.

"Kait, are you sure?" Ethan asked me, stopping to look at me. "Maybe you should get checked out."

I looked back at Ethan and said more confidently, "I'm sure."

"Can I get your statement then?" Officer Quincy asked, all business, despite the too long brown hair.

"Can I give it to you tomorrow? Down at the station?

Or you can call me," I said. I really just wanted to go home.

"I'd prefer to take it now," Officer Quincy said and then continued, shrugging, "It's procedure."

Officer Quincy was just doing his job. He was being nice and all, but I really just wanted to go home. The goo was gross.

I sighed, "Fine. Okay, that kid ran into the funeral viewing room and threw whatever this black stuff is all over me like in a scene from a Stephen King movie or book or whatever. It totally freaked everyone out, including me. Done."

"Well, I have some questions for you, actually..." Officer Quincy said.

"And, I want to answer them," I pleaded. I felt like I was going to start crying if I didn't get out of there. "Tomorrow. I need to get home and get this stuff off of me."

"Okay," Officer Quincy said, "But just a few more minutes, please. Give me your information and let me get a sample of this goo and answer just a few questions for me."

"Fine, briefly," I sighed. He wasn't going to let us leave. I'd better just get it over with.

I answered Officer Quincy's questions as quickly as I could. I mean, I had no idea who'd want to do something like this to me. Although, I did hope the police caught them. It wasn't a pleasant experience at all, getting goo thrown on you and that person deserved to get in trouble. Then I let Officer Quincy take a sample of the goo and some pictures to round out the interview. Even though he said it would only take a few minutes, it still took about forty-five minutes before Officer Quincy let Ethan and I go. It was only after Detective Dixon came over and said that it was okay to let me leave and that he personally knew how to get ahold of me, if the officer needed to. Even after all that, the police still wanted me to come in the next day and elaborate. How many more ways could I tell them that there was no reason anyone should be throwing goo on me at a funeral? I mean, really - was there ever a good reason for that? Especially when I was giving a super awesome speech and for once, wasn't scared to talk to my classmates about how I felt.

I really, really just wanted to go home. This whole thing was only going to add to the gossip about me at school and I was so not thrilled. Finally, Ethan led me away toward the car. It was an awkward ride home. We had to lay down fast food napkins and an old shirt on his car seat, so that I wouldn't get black goo everywhere. At least it seemed like the goo was definitely going to come off. That was a positive.

We drove in silence. My brain was in shock. I felt gross. At least we were at my house before I knew it.

"Is your dad home?" Ethan asked as he put the car in park in my driveway.

The house was dark. My dad was probably over at his friend's house watching a game and hanging out. He did that sometimes after work nowadays.

"I don't think so," I said.

"Do you want me to come in with you?" Ethan asked.

"Yes," I said and started shaking.

Ethan helped me get my keys out of my purse and opened the front door. He led me straight to the bathroom.

"Let me grab a couple of things to try and get this goop off you," Ethan said and disappeared into my house.

I just stood there, wondering how I was going to even

turn the shower on. Ethan was back quickly with olive oil, dish soap, liquid soap, goo be gone, rubbing alcohol, and a few other bottles of cleaner.

"One of these will work. Take a shower and try them," Ethan said and shut the bathroom door for me, so I wouldn't get anything on the door handle.

I peeled off the dirty clothes feeling a little sad that I was probably going to have to throw them away. I looked at the bathtub handles to turn on the water. I was going to have to do it. I turned on the water and the shower. I stepped in and watched the goo pour down the drain.

It took me forever to get it all off. I tried a mixture of the bottles Ethan had brought me, sticking to the more natural stuff. I didn't need to pour more toxic chemicals on my skin. At least I hoped I got it all off. When I stepped out of the shower, the bathroom had turned into a steam room. I wrapped myself in a towel and took a look at myself in the mirror. Most importantly, my face and hair looked squeaky clean.

I looked down at the dirty clothes that I had thrown on the ground. I couldn't put them back on. Yet, the clean clothes were in my room. Okay. Ethan and I weren't at the Kait wears only a towel in front of him stage yet. I couldn't go in there dressed like this. I stared at myself in the mirror. I was suddenly exhausted. I could see it etched into my face. Okay, I was going to go into my room dressed only in a towel and try not to freak out at the implications if my dad happened to come home. I knew nothing was going to happen...yet. I just wasn't sure if I'd suddenly want it to. I mean, kissing Ethan was amazing but more than that just scared the hell out of me.

I opened the bathroom door, peered outside, just in case Ethan happened to be standing there and almost tripped over a pile of neatly folded clean clothes. Ethan must not have been ready to see me in only a towel either. I picked up the clothes gratefully and shut the bathroom door.

When I was fully dressed in the pajamas Ethan had left out for me, hair dripping, and with no makeup, I walked back into my bedroom. Ethan was sitting on my bed. He took one look at me and ran up to hug me. I hugged him back. Then suddenly we were making out. Yes, it was definitely good that I hadn't walked out of the bathroom in just a towel.

Ethan pulled away from me and air rushed between us, "You okay?"

"Yeah," I said, "Just a little spooked. It happened so fast."

"Yeah," Ethan said.

"Have you heard anything? Did they arrest him?" I asked.

"I just texted Dave and Mike. They might still be there, so we'll see if they text back," Ethan said.

"I know that he didn't try to shoot me or anything," I said, "But I'm still super freaked out."

"Yeah, it was so not cool," Ethan said.

I tried to calm my brain down. I was fine. My brain immediately went to the fact that I hadn't had a chance to talk to Ray Newton. If only I hadn't had goo thrown on me. I still needed to check him out.

Ethan's phone beeped. He looked down at his phone and read a text. He frowned and then looked up at me.

"What?" I asked.

Ethan stared at me, "They just charged Seth Wilcox in the murders of Madison Brown and Julia Morgan."

CHAPTER 18
FOOTBALL FOLLOWING

I couldn't sleep all night. Ethan left when my eyes started drooping, which was only around ten pm. I couldn't help it. It had been a long week and I was tired. Getting attacked in the middle of a funeral will do that to you. Of course, as soon as Ethan left and I actually tried to go to sleep, I found that I couldn't.

My dad got home around eleven and I heard him banging around the kitchen. Scarlett, my cat, was fast asleep beside me. My dad was asleep before midnight, if the silence that settled over the house was any indication. I still couldn't sleep. I didn't know what was wrong with me. Thank goodness tomorrow was Saturday and I could sleep in if I wanted to sleep until noon.

My brain didn't want to stop working. I kept going over the details of the case in my head. It just didn't add up to me that Seth Wilcox killed Madison and Julia. I couldn't put my finger on a reason. It was a gut feeling that I had despite the fact that the police discovered that Seth was the one that had thrown goo all over me, *Carrie* style. I didn't know what else the police found when they went to arrest him for that, but there must have been some kind of evidence to connect Seth to the murders.

Still, it didn't sit well with me.

My brain was telling me that Seth was just as bad as Logan said, but I was having a hard time with it. Guess it didn't matter, popular or unpopular, you could still be high school mean to anyone or each other just because. That fit more to me, that Seth was just being a mean idiot by throwing goo on me, than that he'd also committed murder. I just couldn't put my finger on why.

I got out from under the covers, went over to my desk, and turned on my computer. Maybe if I looked Seth up and did more research on him, my brain would settle down, and I'd be able to get to sleep.

I started with Seth's Facebook page. He was definitely anti-school in all respects, but it's that stupid I hate school stuff. I wouldn't have taken it seriously. On the other hand, I could see why the cops might. Some of those kids were legitimately crazy. With Seth, though, it looked like the I'm too cool for school kind of thing, not like the I want to blow up the school and kill people sort. There was a difference. Basically, he didn't look totally insane. There were normal pictures of him and his family and he volunteered at the hospital and just a bunch of things that didn't fit with the I'm a psycopath persona that people wanted to place on him. Sometimes, of course, all of that didn't matter and you had everyone saying - "Wow, I never would have suspected so and so of this, but here they are with the smoking gun." Maybe Seth would turn out to be another example of that, but I wasn't convinced yet.

I looked through Seth's pictures and saw that he had videos. I clicked on the first one and watched as he and his friends pulled a prank on his little brother in *Punk'd* style, where he hid cigarettes in his little brother's room, snitched, and filmed his mom yelling at his brother. The video was posted a couple of months ago. It looked like they had a bunch of similar videos done over the span of a few months, each one was more and more elaborate. The practical jokes were mean, tacky, and tasteless, but maybe last night's *Carrie* moment had been in the same vein and I had been the lucky victim. Only now Seth was facing a murder charge for it.

I went back to bed feeling disgruntled. It still didn't look like Seth committed the murders to me. The problem with that was, if Seth wasn't the murderer then Ariel was still in danger. That was a big problem since I was pretty sure something was going to happen at the football game Saturday night.

I couldn't remember what time I finally fell asleep. It must have been somewhere between five and six am. I had a dull headache from lack of good sleep, regardless. I looked blearily at the time. It was eleven am. I bolted awake. I wasn't supposed to sleep in!

The football game was in a mere seven hours. The Pep Club was meeting at six pm sharp for the six thirty game. We were all going to sit together. I was going to sit next to Ariel, even though I knew she wouldn't want me there, unless I could convince her not to go to the game. Although, somehow I didn't think Ariel would listen to me about that since everyone assumed the killer had been caught.

I turned on my computer and took a look at the latest news on the killings. It was all there: Seth Wilcox arrested for suspicion of murder in the deaths of Madison Brown and Julia Morgan. On paper or on the internet, the guy looked like he was toast. I read a few articles, but they didn't say much. The story was still breaking. Regardless of what the news and the police said, my feeling that Seth hadn't done it persisted.

I grabbed my phone and called Ethan.

"Hello?" I heard him say, sleep still tingeing his voice.

"Hey," I was wide awake. "We need to meet up and investigate some more before the game."

"What do you mean?" Ethan asked.

"I don't think Seth did it," I said.

"What?" Ethan asked, struggling to focus.

"Just get up and meet me at Wired," I said. "I'll see you there by noon. Okay?"

I hung up the phone before Ethan could reply. I had to go and make myself look cute and an hour was barely going to be enough time. Plus, I had to get to Wired, so there was that time commitment to factor in.

I was already sitting at a table with a peanut butter banana milkshake in hand. It was such good comfort food that it almost made everything seem all right, but my nerves were definitely still on edge. Regardless, it was helping, even if just a little.

Ethan saw me, waved, and walked up to the counter to order a coffee. A moment later, he came toward me carrying a steaming mug.

"I need this," Ethan said, taking a sip of his coffee gratefully.

"Long night?" I asked.

Ethan shrugged, "I couldn't sleep, so I messed with some songs."

"I'd love to hear them," I said.

"Sure," Ethan said. "I was actually thinking of maybe going up here sometime. I heard they have an open mic night on Tuesdays."

"Really?" I asked, excited for him. "That would be awesome!"

"Yeah," Ethan said. "I think it's about time I start playing in front of people. You know, before you got that gunk thrown on you at the funeral, your speech really struck a cord with me. It made me think that I need to just do it and put my music out there. I've never seen you put yourself out there like that. It was very inspiring."

I was touched, "Thanks."

"You're welcome," Ethan said and leaned in and quickly kissed me.

This was really nice - an afternoon spent at Wired drinking peanut butter banana milkshakes and coffee with Ethan. Stop! My brain screamed. Murder and Ariel, remember? It was time to get down to business. My notes were in front of me. I had already been looking them over for about ten minutes while I waited for Ethan.

"Okay, onto tonight. I think we need to assume that Seth didn't do it," I said.

"Well, then who did?" Ethan asked. "I mean, the police arrested Seth last night. They must have a good reason."

"Well, as cool as Detective Dixon was to us at the Funeral Home, I don't think he's right in this case," I said.

"We could go talk to him again," Ethan said. "You still have to go down there and continue your statement to the police about last night."

"Yeah," I said. "I would like to do that because I mean, even if he didn't kill anyone, Seth should get in trouble. What if that stuff had gotten into my eye or something? And, I really could have lived without the *Carrie* life moment ever happening to me. Still, I don't think Detective Dixon will change his mind or anything, so it's pointless to do it today."

"What do we do then? We have no idea who else might have done it either," Ethan said, sipping more coffee. I could tell the caffeine was finally waking him up. He seemed to have a little more life around his eyes then when he walked in.

"We investigate some more," I said.

"In the next six hours? What are we going to find?" Ethan asked.

"Well, negative Nancy, we won't find anything if we don't look," I said.

"Negative Nancy? Where did you get that from?" Ethan laughed.

I rolled my eyes, "Who knows. A book? That's not the point."

"Ok, where do you want to start?" Ethan sighed.

"Our list of suspects besides Seth Wilcox, are these four people: Noah Robertson, Sebastian Zane, Jenny Kendall, and Ray Newton," I said.

"But what if it's someone that we haven't suspected yet?" Ethan asked.

"True," I said. "And, it totally could be."

"So, we're basically at square one. Anyone could have done it. Do you have a favorite for the killer?" Ethan asked.

Last time we had argued over the best candidate for murderer. I looked at the list. My number one suspect at first would have been Julia Morgan, but now she was dead too. They all had motives, but were they really enough to make someone commit multiple murders?

"I don't know," I said. "It could be any of them."

"Exactly. We can't follow them all," Ethan said.

An idea lit up like a light bulb in my brain, "Yes, we can!"

"We can?" Ethan asked.

"Here's the plan," I said and proceeded to tell Ethan that since we had four main suspects, all we had to do in the next few hours is to convince four friends to follow them from a safe distance. I'd follow Ariel to keep her safe and Ethan, because it was the only way he'd agree to the plan, would follow me, for the same purpose. Ethan also demanded we see Detective Dixon and tell him about our fears, even if he didn't believe us. I reluctantly agreed.

We started to make the calls to our friends. I was hoping that our friends would just assume that some of the goo from the night before had gone straight to my brain if we were wrong. If we were right, I only hoped nobody got hurt.

It was six pm and Ethan and I were parking his car in the school parking lot. Ethan was a little disgruntled because Detective Dixon hadn't had time to see us. He was off trying to pin the murders on Seth Wilcox. So, I gave my full statement on what happened the night before to Officer Quincy. We also told Officer Quincy our fears, but I could tell he thought we were crazy. I didn't blame him. We were just kids to him, even if he wasn't much older than us. Besides, the police really thought Seth was the murderer. Maybe Seth was, but I couldn't take the chance.

On the upside, a bunch of our friends had agreed to help us follow our murder suspects. I hoped none of them thought I was totally insane, but they had all humored Ethan and I regardless.

That being said, the assignments were as follows: Kyle and Suzie were on Jenny Kendall watch. They were doing their detective work together because they couldn't stand to spend their first football game apart. Gag. I hoped Ethan and I weren't that ridiculous. Still, I was really happy for Kyle and Suzie. I just had to make fun of them so that I wouldn't get weirded out by all of their making out. It was better if it was funny.

Dave was following Sebastian Zane. Mike was

following Ray Newton. I wished I'd had a chance to get to talk to him, but time had run out. I was hoping that he was just a ladies man, but Mike would keep me posted if he did anything weird. They were both keeping an eye on Noah Robertson, since he was supposed to be sitting on the sidelines in his football uniform not playing, and should be relatively easy to spot. Ethan and I were going to keep an eye on him too.

Just to be sure, everyone was also keeping an eye out for Casey Hunt and anybody else who might be suspicious. I wasn't sure if the murderer was in the top few of our list or not and I couldn't take the chance with Ariel's life. I was trying to cover all of our bases. I hoped it was enough.

If anyone heard or saw anything out of the ordinary, they were to text Ethan or I and then call 911. Then they were supposed to get to a safe spot. It was going to be a crazy night, if only just because there were now six of us playing detective and spy.

Ethan and I found the Pep Club. There were already about thirty people waiting with posters, painted faces, and school colored outfits. I was just wearing jeans and a t-shirt and so was Ethan. We hadn't decked ourselves out in school spirit. Oops. I found Ariel pretty quickly in the crowd, lips connected to Troy. At least Troy was also around to protect her. Still, Madison had a date to the Homecoming Dance and he hadn't protected her. I wasn't planning on letting Ariel out of my sight, though, not even to go to the bathroom.

I dragged Ethan toward Ariel and Troy. I had another dejavu moment. It was like our faux double date from a few weeks ago, except the people within the couples were switched. Weird.

"Hey, Ariel. Troy," I said brightly.

Ariel frowned at me, suspiciously, "Hey."

"Hey, Kait. How's it going?" Troy said.

Ethan put his arm around my shoulders.

"Good," I said. "How's the steampunk art?"

"Amazing," Troy gushed, "I was just showing Ariel my latest project today before we drove over here. It's a whole entertainment center. I'm steampunking it out with a bunch of brass and ornamentation, like old clocks and dials. I'm really excited about it. It's going to make my room look amazing and I'm hoping that when I'm done I can take some pictures and maybe start doing it for other people. I'd really like to make my living as an artist. It's the only thing that I really love to do."

"And, he's totally an amazing artist," Ariel stated. "Totally amazing."

Then Ariel kissed him. It was a sloppy kiss and it was kind of gross. I looked at Ethan. He smiled at me and shrugged.

Ariel stepped away from Troy and looked at us, "Anyway, I have to go and be Pep Club president now. Have fun."

Ariel turned to leave. She was going to leave Troy with us and go off on her own. I couldn't let that happen.

"Let me go with you," I said. "I'm part of Pep Club too."

"Uh, okay," Ariel didn't know what to say. "I was just going to go help distribute posters."

"Cool," I said.

Ariel gave me a weird look, but kept walking. She walked over to Mrs. Davis and we helped hand out the rest of the posters that we had made at the meeting to members. I don't think I had ever said hello to so many people in my high school before in all three years put together as I did handing out posters with Ariel and Mrs.

Davis. I'll admit it. It was kind of weird. A lot of the people were actually really friendly. It was disconcerting.

There was a break in the distribution and Ariel turned to me, "Okay, Kait, what's the deal? Why are you following me?"

Wow, it had taken her this long to figure it out? I hesitated - did I warn her or lie? I was bad at lying to Ariel.

"I think you're in danger," I said.

Ariel's eyebrows shot up as she processed this, "But the guy who killed Madison and Julia is in jail."

"I'm not so sure," I said.

"Why?" Ariel asked. "What do you know that the police don't?"

"That's the thing. It's a gut feeling," I said. "I can't prove that Seth didn't do it, but I really don't think he did. I have a lot of other suspects."

Ariel frowned, "And can you prove any of them did it?"

"No," I said. "But it just doesn't add up that Seth did it either. And I'm trying to figure it out, but I think you're in danger tonight. Time ran out. It's another big Pep Club event and..."

"Kait," Ariel said.

"Ariel," I said back. "They haven't signed, sealed, and convicted Seth yet. It could be someone else. Like, do you know Ray Newton?"

"Ray?" Ariel asked. "Madison's ex?"

"Yeah," I said.

"Not really," Ariel said, "I mean, besides Madison complaining about him and how he never did anything romantic for her. Then it was about how he started dating Julia, but kept calling Madison and telling her that he wanted her back. What a jerk."

"Did Madison say anything else about him? Like did he ever hit her or was he super jealous or..." I started.

Ariel sighed, "Kait, just stick to funeral crashing and leave me out of it."

Then Ariel turned her back on me to talk to some members who had come up to get their posters. At least I had learned a little more about Ray. Too bad the time to narrow down suspects was running out. At least between all of Ethan's and my friends we were covered. I watched Ariel's back, silently. It didn't matter if she didn't believe me. My gut was still telling me I was right and that she was in danger.

I tried to keep tabs on Ethan and Troy, who had been left alone together. They had moved toward us and were talking avidly to each other. I sort of wondered what they were talking about. Ethan was so weary of Troy before and now they looked like bffs.

"What do you think they're talking about?" I asked Ariel, who had tried to ignore me for the last ten minutes.

Ariel looked over at Ethan and Troy and frowned too, "I don't know, but I think it's time we get back to them. We're pretty much done with the posters anyway."

I followed Ariel back over to Ethan and Troy. Their conversation stopped short as soon as we approached. That was interesting.

"So, were you guys talking about us?" Ariel asked, using her seductive voice.

I thought it was funny, but Troy was suddenly sliding toward Ariel, in response.

"We were just talking," Ethan grinned.

"You're not gonna tell us, are you?" I asked.

"Nope," Ethan said.

Troy and Ariel started making out again. I would have dragged Ethan as far away from them as possible, but we had a pact to watch Ariel. If she got murdered because I couldn't stand some of the uncomfortableness of watching her makeout with Troy, I'd never forgive myself.

"So," Ethan said, staring at me wide-eyed, trying not to notice what was happening next to us.

"So," I responded staring back at him.

This was so totally awful that I had to force my limbs to stay put and not run away screaming. How were we going to do this all night? I couldn't take one more minute, much less hours of this!

"Okay, everyone! Let's head off to the stands! It would be great for the group to sit together, but if you sit with your friends, just remember to show your school spirit! Support your team!" Mrs. Davis said. "Ariel, do you want to say anything?"

Ariel stopped making out with Troy just in time to pay attention to Mrs. Davis, "Go Palos Grizzlies!"

The group cheered. Ariel had that effect on people. Minimal effort and yet she still got an amazing response. It was definitely a talent.

There were about fifty Pep Club members in attendance and they surrounded us as we walked to the bleachers. I pulled Ethan along and tried to keep pace with Ariel and Troy, so that we wouldn't lose them in the crowd. We absolutely had to sit next to them, as horrific as that sounded after watching them make out for only a minute. It was a necessary evil.

I probably lost some of the friends I made handing out posters with Ariel because I pushed and shoved my way through the crowd repeatedly to keep pace with her. For some reason, Ariel kept moving this way and that, like she was trying to lose me. Oh who was I kidding? Ariel was totally trying to shake me, but it wasn't going to happen if I had anything to say about it. I was sticking to Ariel like glue. Cliché or not it was true.

Ariel ran up the bleachers with Troy in tow, glancing around frantically for a place to sit so that she could get away from me. I could almost see the wheels in her brain turning, trying to figure out how to dodge me next.

"Hey, Ariel, come sit with us," Logan said to them.

I saw that Logan was sitting with a few other popular people, including Sebastian Zane. Dave was where he was supposed to be, two rows up and watching his target. Dave waved to Ethan and me. Ethan waved back at him. Dave was getting a kick out of the whole thing. At least one of us was having fun.

Ariel looked over at us triumphantly - the row was packed! She scooted her way into the middle, with Troy following. People made room for them. There really was no room left on that row of bleachers, but Ethan and I had to sit there. I couldn't take the chance that I'd miss Ariel get up and leave to go somewhere.

"What are we going to do?" Ethan asked, following my gaze.

In response, I grabbed his hand and started climbing over people toward Ariel.

"I'm not going to be very popular after this," Ethan whispered in my ear, stepping on someone's foot and apologizing.

I had given up on apologizing. I was about to push two people out of their seats and onto the floor. Oh well. They could add rude to my reputation. It probably already included goo girl, although nobody had said anything to me about that yet. Maybe it was because Ethan was at my side. They wouldn't dare make fun of me in front of him since I appeared to be his girl. Was I? He was too cute and too popular to get taunted, at least to his face, and while I was with him, I was safe.

"Hey, Troy!" I said brightly, climbing over one last person, "Can we sit here?"

Troy looked surprised. He hadn't noticed the great chase that had just occurred, "Sure."

I sat down in the tiny space Troy offered me next to him and pulled Ethan down beside me and almost into some guy's lap.

"Whoa," Ethan said, almost falling onto me.

People complained, but I pretended I didn't hear them and focused on Troy. Ethan settled in next to me.

"Thanks, Troy!" I said. "Hey, Logan!"

"Hey," Logan smiled. Wow, did he have a smile on him.

Ariel shot me daggers. Wait a minute. She couldn't possibly be interested in Logan when Troy was sitting next to her, right?

"I was just telling Ariel that Seth Wilcox is out on bail. I wonder if he'll show up here tonight," Logan said.

"What?" I asked.

"That's what I heard," Logan said.

"He's not going to show up here," Ariel said, looking at me pointedly.

It was great that she was so unconcerned, being the Pep Club president and possibly the next target. My mind was racing. We needed to keep an eye out for Seth now too, just in case, even if I was half sure it wasn't him. It would be stupid of him to show up at the game, in fact, but hey, he might be that dumb if he was willing to pull a *Carrie* style prank at a funeral.

I turned to Ethan, "Text Dave and Mike to keep a lookout for Seth. I'll text Suzie."

Ethan nodded. We both pulled out our phones. By the time I looked up, Ariel had turned her back on me and started talking to Logan. Wow, she was willing to ignore her date because of me. That was okay. I liked Troy. I was happy to talk to him.

"So, Troy tell me more about your steampunk project," I said.

I saw Ariel's back stiffen. She knew Troy couldn't resist the bait. Troy started talking. It was interesting hearing the intricate details of each piece he was planning to use in his project and I really was intrigued, but I had to pay attention to Ariel, the general atmosphere, and the phone in my pocket in case I got a text or a call. Oh, and I had to at least remember to pay some attention to Ethan, who I had my back to because I was talking to Troy. Still, Ethan was kind of my date to the game, even if we were playing follow your target. I reached behind me and squeezed Ethan's hand.

Ethan's breath was in my ear, "This is awful."

I grinned and nodded at something Troy said, "That sounds totally amazing."

Troy kept talking to me. Ariel kept talking to Logan. Ethan kept breathing in my ear.

"I'd much rather have spent tonight going on a date with you," Ethan whispered.

I wanted to lean back against Ethan, as Troy droned on. I would much rather have been on a real date too, but I had to stay alert and keep focused. I had to take notice of things like that Ariel was walking down toward the concession stand and not in her seat anymore.

CHAPTER 19
MURDER SOLVING

Wait. What? Ariel was already almost down the bleachers. How had I not seen her get up? She hadn't even bothered to tell Troy. She was probably mad at him. I felt bad for Troy. I hadn't meant to get him in trouble with his girl.

"Uh, sorry to interrupt, Troy, but I need to go and talk to Ariel!" I said, letting go of Ethan's hand and jumping over Troy, Logan, Sebastian, and countless others in my race to keep up with Ariel.

Troy didn't even have a chance to respond, but I did see the surprised look on his face as he realized Ariel wasn't sitting next to him anymore. I didn't even wait for Ethan to join me. He was probably just as surprised that I was sprinting off as Troy was. I ran full barrel toward Ariel. She moved fast. Ariel was already almost at the concession stand by the time I made it out of the row. I tried to keep my eyes trained on her. The game was going to start in the next few minutes and the whole area was suddenly packed with students.

In the glow of the stadium lights and at a distance, it was hard to tell differentiate between people and it was hard keeping track of which girl was Ariel. As soon as I reached the bottom of the bleachers, I broke into a run. I couldn't afford to lose her. People swore at me and called me names and I knew I was only adding more and more to my freak reputation as I pushed past people walking toward the stands in my race to get to Ariel. It ceased to matter to me.

I reached the concession stand. Ariel was nowhere to be seen. I scanned the lines again. There was a bustle of activity, but no Ariel. I was pretty sure she wasn't there. I scanned again. No, she was definitely not there. There were bathrooms down the way inside the school. I ran. I did not want anyone to find Ariel like they had found Madison.

I saw Jenny Kendall in the concession line, flanked by Kyle and Suzie, who were holding hands. They seemed to be having an amazing time with each other despite the situation. At least they were actually keeping tabs on their target. They didn't notice me. They were too absorbed in themselves, with occasional glances at Jenny.

How had they managed to keep such good tabs on Jenny with those googly eyes at each other, when I had only looked away from Ariel for an instant and she had disappeared? It wasn't fair. I wanted to be making googly eyes at Ethan instead of chasing after my ex-best friend.

I burst into the bathroom and pushed open and looked in all of the stalls. I was definitely not making any friends tonight, I thought, as I almost opened the door on someone actually using the bathroom. Oops. Ariel was not in any of them. Where was she? I felt frantic. I couldn't believe I had lost her. I was so careful.

I ran out of the bathroom, even more frantic. The game had just started. People were everywhere. How was I going to find Ariel in this crowd? I tried to look over at our seats, wondering if she had somehow circled around me and made it back without me seeing her. I couldn't tell. It was like distinguishing ants from a distance. I just saw a sea of school colors.

I looked over toward the football team. Was Noah where he was supposed to be? His number was 57. I thought I saw him sitting on the bench. I hoped the others were keeping tabs on him. I had to find Ariel.

I started back, weaving through the crowds and making more enemies in my mad rush to find Ariel. Then I saw her. She was standing near the fence at the back of the bleachers, where it was out of the way and more than a little in shadow. I could only tell it was her because of the distinctive Ariel stance I knew so well. Didn't Ariel know that you didn't go off by yourself into dark scary recesses of, well, anywhere, when there might be a killer on the loose? I had even warned her! She was probably making out or about to with Troy, which was gross, but I had to get her back into the crowd. She'd be safe in a sea of people.

I ran toward her. Ariel was definitely talking to someone in the shadows, but I couldn't see who because the darkness was covering their face. I kept running. My eyes were focused on Ariel, but I was still trying to discern who she was talking to, in the hopes that it was only Troy. She'd be safe with Troy.

As I got closer, I could see that the person Ariel was talking to had on jeans and red sneakers. Red. They looked like high tops. Were they Chuck Taylor's? A burst of adrenaline shot through me and I found myself running faster.

My phone was in my hand and I was dialing Ethan.

"Kait! Where are you?" Ethan's voice screamed into the phone.

"Behind the bleachers. Ariel. Killer. Call the police," I

gasped back without waiting for him to say anything else.

It would be embarrassing if I was wrong, but I didn't care. I had to keep running. I was almost there. I pushed past a last crowd of people, losing sight of my target for a moment. I finally got around them and ran toward Ariel, except now she wasn't there. A chill fell over me. Where was she? I looked frantically around the spot she had been standing. They must have gone under the bleachers. I had to get to Ariel.

I ran over to the spot where Ariel had been standing. A short fence with a gate prevented you from entering, but I could see that the gate was slightly ajar. Shafts of light fell through the bleachers into the dark recesses below them. It took my eyes a moment to adjust. I couldn't hear anything due to the screaming and talking of the students above me. This really was the perfect place to commit a murder.

Then my eyes adjusted and there they were. A shaft of light was hitting Ariel's big nose. Okay, it wasn't that big. I could almost see the killer's red sneakers glowing ominously, but it might have been my imagination too. I was on red alert.

I really hoped the police were coming because I was about to do something nobody should ever do in this situation. Ever. I couldn't help myself, though, I had to try and save her. I hoped Ariel stopped gossiping about me after this or at least said nice things, if we survived the situation.

I did my best to stealthily creep toward them, from behind the killer. I still couldn't see any defining detail about who it was from where I was standing, except for the bright red shoes.

"Please, don't do this," Ariel said. "I won't tell. I haven't done anything to you. I'll...I'll resign from Pep

Club even."

I could finally hear them. Ariel was freaking out. I could hear the panic in her voice. I had to help her.

"I don't care about the Pep Club," he said.

Wait. It was a guy. It was most definitely a male voice and I recognized it. Where did I recognize it? Oh. My. Gawd. It was Logan Collins, the hottest most popular guy in school, well, next to Ethan, at least to me. He hadn't even made my list! I was the worst sleuth ever - taken in by a guy's hotness and duped into not even considering him as a suspect. It just goes to show, looks really do help you out in life and that you can't trust looks at all. His ex-best friend Seth was totally right and Seth had almost gone down for the murders, despite that.

Now, Logan was trying to kill Ariel. If this wasn't happening right in front of my eyes, I wouldn't have believed it. Yes, it was dark, but still. Why was Logan Collins a murderer? He had everything, well, I mean, everything popularity gave you which in high school was, well, everything.

I moved forward. I was creeping up right behind Logan. He was still focused on Ariel and she was mesmerized. It was like watching one of those videos on YouTube where an animal is poised, waiting to pounce on its prey. Neither of them had seen me yet, maybe because they were so focused on each other or maybe because the darkness was on my side.

"Then why are you doing this?" Ariel asked. "I barely even know you! I mean, I thought maybe you like liked me or something, although I am dating Troy, but I guess not. I mean..."Logan laughed, "It doesn't matter why."

"But at least tell me, I mean, if you're gonna kill me, why do I have to die?" Ariel was rambling.

I could tell that Ariel was trying to stall for time,

hoping that help was on the way. I hoped so too. Ethan had heard me, right? He was calling the police? They knew where we were? I couldn't worry about it now. It was too late if he hadn't. What was happening between Logan and Ariel was going to happen in minutes, maybe seconds. I was the only one that had a chance to intervene.

Logan laughed again, "Would you believe that I have made one mistake in my whole life and that I've been paying for it ever since?"

"A mistake? What mistake?" Ariel asked.

As I quietly crept forward, glad for the cheers and screams above me, covering up any noise I was making, I started to wonder what on earth I was planning to do once I did come up behind Logan. Should I jump him? I was guessing he had a gun or something trained on Ariel, although I couldn't see it. What else could I do? I couldn't just let him shoot her or stab her or whatever he was planning to do. Maybe then if Ariel helped me, we could wrestle him to the ground. There wasn't much time to plan this all out, unfortunately.

Logan kept laughing, so it almost sounded like a joke, but he was deadly serious, "I got Madison Brown pregnant in junior high."

"What?" Ariel asked. I could tell she was completely floored from the way her voice rose an octave, "Madison had a baby? Are you serious?"

If I hadn't been so focused on trying to save Ariel, I would have frozen in my tracks. Madison had a baby? My blood turned cold. Lana. She was the spitting image of Madison. Logan wouldn't try to kill her too, would he?

"She had her right before freshman year. Her sister, Lana, is her daughter. Nobody knew. Except Julia. Madison told her. Told her that I was the dad. Nobody else knew who the father was, not even Madison's parents. I made Madison promise not to tell. Then, all of a sudden, Madison wanted to tell Lana the truth about everything. She wanted to tell her that she was her mother and that I was her father," Logan said. "My parents couldn't find out. The school couldn't find out. Nobody could find out. I worked so hard to get where I am. I was a pimple-faced kid with braces and glasses at the start of junior high. I was flattered Madison Brown even wanted to be more than friends. I was stupid to make the mistake I did. I've been smarter ever since, but I just keep paying for it. It had to go away, so I killed Madsion."

I thought about little Lana, the poor girl. I hoped she never found out who her father was and I wasn't normally an advocate for that sort of thing. I mean, I think you should always have access to that sort of information. Like, if I was adopted, I'd want to know. In this case, though, that sweet little girl who just lost her sister/mom didn't deserve to know that her dad did it. It could mess a little kid up. Too bad in the real world, when this all got out, she'd probably be on CNN or some other talk show with her grandparents. I really hoped her grandparents got her out of town when it happened instead. That would really be the best thing for her.

"Why did you kill Julia then?" Ariel asked. Her plan to stall for time was working so far.

Logan laughed again. It was a really creepy laugh, "Well, for starters, Julia knew I killed Madison. She helped me do it. We planned it together."

"What?" Ariel was shocked again.

I knew it! Well, I had thought for a second at least that Julia's involvement in Madison's murder made sense. She had acted really strange the day she talked to me. Julia would have been my prime suspect, had she not been killed too. Logan had thrown me off that scent, by killing her.

"Julia wanted Madison dead for different reasons. The whole thing was Julia's idea, actually. She'd get the Pep Club presidency and get even with Madison for taking everything she wanted away from her. Julia would get back her high school status. Madison really did a number on Julia's reputation. Maybe there was more to it. I didn't care. Once Julia suggested it to me, I was in. Like I said, I needed Madison gone too," Logan said.

"So you both did it?" Ariel asked. She was having a hard time with the concept.

It made a lot of sense to me, though. Popularity was worth a lot to some people. I mean, in high school, your status was everything.

"Yeah, it was so easy. We hid in the bathroom during the Homecoming Dance and waited," Logan said.

"But what if we hadn't gone to the bathroom?" Ariel asked. "Or even that bathroom?"

"According to Julia, it was a sure thing. Madison had the smallest bladder and she preferred that particular bathroom because less people used it, which made it less disgusting or some OCD thing like that, so Julia said that Madison was sure to show up," Logan said. "And, it was likely to be for the most part deserted since it was out of the way."

"But what if someone found you?" Ariel asked.

Logan shrugged, "Then we'd pretend to be making out in the stall and try again later. Otherwise, once it was done, we'd blend into the crowd. There were hundreds of people at the dance. It was a perfect place to blend in and commit murder. So, we waited and twenty minutes in, you guys walked into the bathroom. It was fate."

"Would you have killed me too?" Ariel wanted to know.

I felt a chill crawl up my spine. I wouldn't have been able to save Ariel. I wouldn't have known until it was too late. I had to save her now. Should I try and wait for the police? Did I just jump him?

Logan continued his story, "Yes, we would have killed you both, collateral damage, but you left in time. We burst out of the stall and confronted Madison. I covered the bathroom door and Julia was supposed to shoot Madison. That was the plan. Julia wanted to do it. We were going to blame it on someone's anti-school spirit, one of the school outcasts, like Seth. He was perfect. People like him practically dressed the part."

"So, Seth had nothing to do with it at all?" Ariel asked.

"No," Logan laughed. "He's perfect, though, right?"

Poor Seth. He was all too perfect to be accused and he might have even been convicted. I couldn't help but be captivated by what Logan was saying. It was horrifying. Yet, I was also multitasking. I had about a minute or two until I would probably have to act. I didn't think the police were going to arrive before Logan tried to kill Ariel. It was up to me. I crept forward. I was almost there.

"So what happened then?" Ariel asked instead of answering Logan's question.

"At the last minute, Julia couldn't do it. So, I did it. I followed through. We got away with it too. Nobody even looked at us for the murder. Madison's death wasn't enough for Julia, though. She was getting the Pep Club presidency, but she wanted more. So, she threatened to expose me as the murderer. She'd claim that she was the innocent victim. Julia wanted things from me. She said I had to date her and do all of these things for her or she would tell people about my daughter, the murder, everything. Julia wanted to be even more popular than she'd been before. I finally got the impression that Julia set me up. I had been stupid. I shouldn't have trusted her. She had it all planned. If anyone found out what we had done, she would make sure that I did the time for it. Julia hadn't been scared to shoot Madison. She had been playing me for a fool. Julia didn't want to be the one to shoot the gun, so that she could point her finger at me, if we were found out. I was smarter in the end, though. We had already given the cops the idea that anti-Pep Club sentiment was the reason for the murder, so I decided to make it the reason for two murders," Logan said.

I couldn't believe the story Logan was weaving, but from what I knew of Julia, I'd believe it of her. They were equally as crazy. The only innocent victims here were Madison and of course, Lana.

"But I didn't know about any of this. I didn't know that either of you killed Madison or that you had a daughter or anything," Ariel said. "Why are you doing this to me?"

"You know now," Logan pointed out.

"But I didn't know five minutes ago," Ariel argued.

I was right behind Logan. Did I wait a little longer? Maybe the police were coming? Did I act? I was scared.

"Well, I have heard rumors that you might have seen me before I killed Madison," Logan said. "Julia was worried that you might have seen something too. Better safe than sorry and all that."

"I didn't," Ariel replied, but all of us could tell she was lying.

"Sure you didn't," Logan said. "But at this point, it doesn't matter, does it? Besides, you fit the pattern now. It works to kill you. It all fell into place. It was meant to be."

"But you don't have to," Ariel pleaded.

"Yes, I do. I helped kill Madison to get rid of one problem. Then Julia started in on me, so I had to get rid of her too. Nobody was going to pull my strings. The whole Pep Club murders gave both of their deaths credibility, like a serial killer had done it. Seth was already arrested once and I'm going to make sure they lock him up for it. He's here, you know. I baited him to come and if I kill you, the investigation will definitely focus on him and his anti-school spirit."

"Wow," Ariel said.

I was having trouble believing it all myself. Logan was insane. Was there something in the water in Palos lately?

"Yeah," Logan said. "You're gonna have to die."

With those words, I knew there were only seconds left to act. The police had not shown up. Neither had Ethan or any of our friends, although I was glad for that. I didn't want to put any more people I cared about in danger.

I took a deep breath, steeled my nerves as much as I could, and jumped on Logan's back, screaming. Ariel froze. I could see her wondering if she had just been shot. Logan had not fired the gun, thank goodness, so her shock was misplaced. Logan, had in fact dropped the gun, as I attacked him and was now trying to pull me off of his back as I did what damage I could with my hands, while also holding onto him tightly.

"Get off me!" Logan yelled. "Get off me!"

He didn't know it was me, Kait Lenox, on his back. Good looks wouldn't save him now. I wish I had started on those self defense classes I had been thinking about. I should do that once this was all over. I seemed to be getting into a lot of dangerous scrapes lately. It would be a useful tool to have on my belt. In the meantime, I had

Ariel to help me in my fight, if only she'd snap out of her daze.

"Get the gun, Ariel!" I screamed.

I wasn't sure if she heard me or not. Ariel was still standing there like a zombie. I knew she wasn't hurt.

"Ariel! Get the gun!" I yelled again.

Logan was scratching at my arms now with his hands, as well as trying to shake me off. I was going to have some serious scratches once this was all over. That wasn't good. I didn't want scars on my arms.

"Ariel! The gun!" I yelled.

Logan dug into my arms with his nails. I screamed. That really hurt. I knew I was bleeding. I had to hold on. I could not let go. Ariel was still standing there blankly. If I let go, Logan would shoot us both. I could not let go.

"Ariel!" I yelled.

Ariel finally snapped out of it and saw me. Recognition registered on her face. Finally. That was the last thing I saw as Logan shook us both to the ground in some kind of wrestling move. I felt the side of my face hit the pavement. That was going to leave a huge bruise. At least I hadn't landed on my nose. I struggled against Logan. Self defense classes were definitely at the top of my list. I tried to knee Logan in the groin, like they did in all of those movies, but it's harder than it looks when you're also wrestling around and fighting for your life. Logan was on top of me, wrestling with my hands, and I couldn't get the impact I wanted in that area. He groaned, but didn't let go of me. We fought on.

I couldn't see what Ariel was doing, but I could only hope that she had registered the words - gun and get it and was doing just that. There was nothing more I could do about the situation than continue fighting Logan with every reserve of energy that I had left.

He was going to kill me. I could almost see the obituary now - *Kait Lenox, 16, killed by the most popular, good looking senior boy at Palos High died Saturday. She is survived by her father, William Lenox, and her cat, Scarlett. Oh, and she crashed funerals.* And, there better be something in there about Ethan Ripley and the word girlfriend too. Oh, and Ariel better cry at the funeral. It was the least I deserved for trying to save her life even though we were ex-bffs.

I couldn't die. I bit Logan's arm. He screamed. I meant for it to hurt. What was Ariel doing? I couldn't even look for her. All of my energy was on keeping Logan's hands and feet from doing severe damage. He was sweating and his face was contorted with this weird look. It was really kind of creepy, actually. Maybe he wasn't that hot at all. I fought on.

I needed to have a serious talk with Ariel when this was all over about listening. I mean, when I said, "Ariel get the gun!" what did she think I meant, you know? I meant - Ariel, get the gun! I was going to kill her if Logan didn't end up killing us both first.

"Freeze!" I finally heard Ariel yell, like she was in a movie.

Logan didn't freeze, so neither did I. He must not have believed Ariel would shoot the gun. I hoped Ariel did. I didn't want to get shot again, by accident, but I was starting to lose this battle. My arms really hurt from all of the scratches and fighting with Logan. The side of my face was swelling up and I was getting a massive headache. If this all didn't end soon, I was going to be in major trouble.

"Stop or I'll shoot!" Ariel tried again, taking another line from a movie.

Ariel really wasn't good at this stopping our fighting thing. Then again, I wasn't surprised. This wasn't the sort of thing Ariel would normally be doing on a Saturday night. She'd be happier at the mall or on a date or actually watching the football game with the rest of the school. I was the one that had chosen to investigate and pursue this murder case. I might have to rethink that path myself if I made it out of this alive.

Logan was still not listening to Ariel. My arms were definitely weakening. He managed to pin them to the side with one hand and his other hand was reaching for my throat.

Ariel shot the gun. Logan jumped. Even I was surprised. Logan didn't topple off of me like I wanted him to. She hadn't shot him. I didn't think Ariel had shot me by accident either. At least, I wasn't feeling pain or bleeding. And it didn't sound like Ariel shot it into the stands because nobody was screaming or anything up there. All I heard was chanting, talking, and sports yelling. Other than that, the voice of the announcer was drowning all sound out. Ariel must have shot it into the dirt.

Logan was distracted enough, though, that I managed to get my hands out of his grip. He turned back to me and started fighting again. We were in a death match.

"Stop!" Ariel screamed again. "Logan Collins, I will shoot you! I swear!"

Logan must not have believed her. I suddenly did, though. I had heard that voice before. It was her determined voice. Ariel always used it when she wasn't getting her way and then she used that voice and voila! Suddenly, Ariel Walker got her way. In this case, all she had to do was pull the trigger.

I heard the bang of the gun. I braced myself for accidentally getting shot. My guess was that it was only the second time in her life Ariel had fired a gun and I wouldn't have been surprised if she shot me instead of Logan. Then I saw Logan's face above mine. This shock was different from the first one. This shock was the - Oh no, I'm hurt, I'm shot kind. I remembered that feeling all too well.

We might just make it out of this alive. There was hope! I saw Logan reach for his upper left leg and his hand came back bloody. Ariel had shot him in the leg! She had actually hit her target! Go, Ariel! My esteem for her just rose a few points.

Ariel was screaming. She was holding the gun at her side and yelling. She was in shock. I was in shock too because I had only just noticed that she was freaking out. Then again, Logan was still on top of me, trying to assess his injuries.

"Ariel! Put the gun back on him!" I yelled.

Ariel kept screaming. The next thing I knew, Logan had climbed off of me and was running at Ariel in a burst of adrenaline and fury. He was going to kill her. I ignored the pain shooting up my arms and in my face and neck and got up to run after him.

"Freeze! Police!" Detective Dixon yelled.

I froze. Ariel froze. Logan did not. There was another gunshot. I hit the ground and so did Ariel. Logan tried to, but the shot was aimed at him. It hit him in the same leg and he went down. That had to hurt. Ariel bolted for safety toward the police and away from Logan. I stayed where I was on the ground. I just wanted to go to sleep. Logan was writhing in pain. From my spot on the floor, I saw Detective Dixon and a bunch of policemen walking toward us. Ethan was behind them. My savior. I could relax now. I passed out.

CHAPTER 20
STATUS LEARNING

I woke up in the hospital. Again. Was this going to be a bi-monthly event? My dad was so going to kill me. He had complained about the previous hospital bills, but then maintained that he was proud of me for sticking to my gut instincts and supporting Ethan in the search for his half sister's killer despite what anyone else thought. I wasn't so sure he was going to feel the same this time. Although, maybe I'd get some points for saving Ariel's life. My parents had liked her as much as her parents had liked me. So, maybe that was worth something.

I looked around the room. Nobody was in my room with me. I felt my heart plummet. Last time I woke up, Ethan was by my side. It was like a romance novel, except real, and then he had stayed with me for almost the whole time I was in the hospital, except for the sleeping parts. Where was he? I knew I saw him coming to my rescue...right?

Then as if on cue, there was Ethan, in the doorway with flowers. They were sunflowers and I had never seen a more beautiful sight. I had never gotten flowers from anyone other than my parents before in my entire life. In fact, I think the last time I got flowers from them was for my eighth grade graduation and they were red roses. They made it through an entire week without dying on the desk in my bedroom. This was the first time I was ever getting them from a boy, though. Particularly, a boy I really, really, really like liked.

I'll admit it. It was pretty cool. I hurt all over, particularly my arms and my head, but my stomach was suddenly full of happy butterflies and I don't think I've ever felt so great. Well, except maybe at the Homecoming Dance when Ethan and I were dancing, before all the crazy stuff happened. Or, when Ethan kissed me the first time. Okay, it was definitely in the top five moments of my life.

"Hey, you," Ethan said, walking in.

"Hey," I squeaked.

"Your dad's outside making some calls, do you want me to go and get him?" Ethan asked.

"No, it's okay," I said. "You're here."

"Okay. These are for you then," Ethan said as he walked over to me and put the flowers on my bedside table. "I was going to go for roses, you know, the whole romantic flower thing, but these reminded me of you more because they're bright and sunny and amazing. I know you like funerals and maybe black roses would have been more appropriate and more you to most people, but to me, you're like a bunch of sunflowers. You brighten my life."

I smiled. I was glad it didn't hurt to smile. I reached for Ethan's hand and he placed his in mine. I could see now that my arms were wrapped in gauze. I hoped the scratches wouldn't turn into scars. I had a boy to look cute for now.

"Thank you," I said. "They're the best flowers ever."

Ethan smiled, "I'm glad you like them. Just promise me that the next time I get you flowers, it won't be because you're in the hospital, okay?"

"I promise," I said. "I'm totally done with this whole hospital thing. It's totally overrated."

"Glad I'm finally getting through to you on that, at least," Ethan said.

I smiled and we stared at each other for a moment. Ethan bent down and lightly kissed me on the lips. I tried to kiss him back, but he pulled away.

"What's wrong?" I asked.

"I just don't want to hurt you," Ethan said.

"I'm fine," I said, wanting to kiss him some more. "Really."

Ethan turned serious, "Kait, it's really scary to almost lose you."

I nodded, "I'm really sorry."

"Don't go off like that again," Ethan said.

"I had to save Ariel," I said. "She is okay, right?"

"She's freaked out and in shock, but physically she's fine. Troy's with her," Ethan said.

"Good," I said and felt a weight lift off my chest. Ariel was okay. I had saved her.

"She wants to see you," Ethan said.

"She does?" I was surprised.

"Yeah," Ethan said.

"Wow, okay," I said. I figured Ariel would probably be milking the attention from Troy and everyone else for all it was worth instead of wanting to talk to me, "Why?"

Ethan shrugged and then said, "My guess is that she wants to say thank you for saving her life."

I nodded, silent. Ariel didn't need to thank me. I couldn't not save her. Even if we weren't friend friends, Ariel still meant something to me.

"What happened to Logan?" I asked. "What happened in general? I mean, I seem to pass out after everything finally goes down and miss all the best parts."

Ethan laughed, "Well, you called me. I freaked. I called the police. Detective Dixon came straight here and we found you guys under the bleachers. He shot Logan, who's now in the hospital. There are reporters all over the place. This story totally beat out my sister's. Poor Lana Brown. Logan confessed to everything as the police handcuffed him."

"Wow," I said. "So, have the Browns made a statement? Are they going to do a paternity test?"

Ethan shook his head, "As far as I can tell they bolted out of town. I'm guessing they're trying to help keep Lana safe."

"Good," I said. "That little girl totally doesn't deserve this insanity. What about Julia's parents?"

"They released a statement basically saying that their daughter was murdered by a maniac and it was an insult to her memory that anyone would believe a word he said about their daughter," Ethan said.

"Wow," I managed. "Sadly, I think they're wrong. There was definitely something off with her."

"Maybe, but I'm still having a hard time believing any of it. It's just so crazy. I sort of knew Logan Collins. He never struck me as a murderer. Ever. It's freaking me out," Ethan said.

"Well, just the thought that Madison had a baby the summer before freshman year and that people thought she was just getting fat is crazy," I said.

"Yeah," Ethan said, "It's totally nuts, but they've got a confession from him, so Logan will probably go to jail for quite a while. He's only seventeen, though, but maybe they'll charge him as an adult. He did kill two people and tried to kill two more."

"I hope so," I said.

"And, by the way, we got some reports back from our other sleuths," Ethan said.

"Really?" I asked.

"Yeah, they took their jobs pretty seriously," Ethan said.

"What did they say?" I asked. I was curious. Plus, I was kind of impressed that they had taken the time to report to us.

"Kyle and Suzie said that Jenny Kendall did absolutely nothing unusual except eat a lot of junk food, like two hotdogs, nachos, and soda. They actually wrote down everything she ate," Ethan said.

I almost laughed. Kyle and Suzie had wanted to give me details, even if it meant giving me Jenny Kendall's junk food preferences.

Ethan continued, "More helpful, they also wrote down everyone Jenny talked to, including Sebastian Zane. Kyle and Suzie eavesdropped on their conversation. It sounded to them like Jenny and Sebastian were plotting to overthrow Ariel," Ethan said. "Step one was to complain that Ariel wasn't with the other Pep Club members being all presidenty."

I chimed in, "Of course, they didn't know that she was busy almost getting murdered."

"Yeah," Ethan said. "And Dave and Mike decided to team up. Dave left Sebastian once Kyle and Suzie were watching him and Jenny plot their takeover of the Pep Club. They got bored watching Ray hook up with a girl in the stands. In Mike's words: They didn't come up for air for twenty minutes. They decided Ray wasn't the killer. He was just a player. So, then they took it upon themselves to chat with Noah Robertson when Dave caught him in the bathroom without his cast on."

"What did Noah say?" I asked.

"He confessed to a whole lot, actually. Noah faked the injury to get out of playing football and he went so far as to fake being angry at Madison about the whole thing for months. He just didn't want to play football and his dad wouldn't let him quit. He didn't want to play in college. Then he was afraid people would think he was the murderer because he had acted so angry at Madison," Ethan said.

So Noah did have the cast on the wrong foot! I had at least, noticed something off about that. I was really impressed with everybody's efforts. We all made a great team.

"Can you tell them that they all did a really great job?" I asked. I was really impressed, actually. They had backed me up...like friends.

"Already did," Ethan said. "So, Ariel?"

"What about her?" I asked.

"She wanted to come in and talk to you," Ethan reminded me.

"Right now?" I asked. "I thought you meant one day or someday or something."

"Right now," Ethan said. "I told her I would get her once you woke up."

I felt Ethan's hand in mine. I didn't want to let it go. I did want to see Ariel, though, just to make sure that she was really okay.

"Alright," I said. "Send her in, but then come back, okay?"

"I will be right outside," Ethan said.

I nodded. Ethan left. I looked at the flowers on my bedside table. Ethan was really an amazing and supportive boyfr...guy. I couldn't say the boyfriend word yet, I reminded myself. Surely the flowers were a step in the right direction, though, right? I thought so. I mean, I had never gotten flowers from any other guy besides my dad, after all.

I was still looking at the flowers when Ariel walked in. I was surprised. She was normally the epitome of the words well coifed and she looked totally disheveled. She walked toward me, as if in a daze and collapsed in the chair next to my bed. I was surprised to see that she then grabbed my hand and peered into my face.

"Are you okay?" Ariel asked and there was actual worry in her eyes.

I had scared Ariel by almost dying. I mean, I knew I was affected by her almost getting murdered, but somehow flipping the sentiment and having Ariel feel that way about me totally freaked me out. So, she actually kind of sort of still cared about me? Weird.

"I'm alright," I managed to say, although suddenly there was this ball stuck in my throat and I felt my eyes prickling with tears.

What in the world was wrong with me? Why was I about to cry? Especially, why was I about to cry in front of Ariel?

Ariel nodded, tears in her eyes too, "I just wanted to say thank you for coming to find me and saving me from that psycopath. I know I haven't been the nicest person to you in the last few years, but I really appreciate that. And, um, I'm sorry."

I nodded. I didn't know what to say. You're welcome? It seemed too formal.

"And, um, you're really okay and all, you know, just so you know," Ariel kept talking.

An okay from Ariel regarding me was about the same as her telling me I was an awesome person. I was floored.

Wow, all I needed to get back on Ariel's good side was to save her life. Another part of me wondered how long this would last. Surely, once she got back to her normal life, Ariel would forget all about me and go back to the popular crowd.

Ariel continued, "And, I wanted to say, um, maybe we could go get peanut butter banana milkshakes at Wired sometime like we used to? You know? Just talk like old times if you're okay with that."

Okay, now I was really floored. Ariel wanted to go get peanut butter banana milkshakes with me at Wired? Where someone might see her? And, yes, that used to be one of our things when we were friends - drinking peanut butter banana milkshakes together since we had discovered them together, but wow, I was surprised that she had brought that up. Ariel could have just stuck with the - I'm sorry and thank you and I would have been pretty impressed.

"That sounds fun," I said once I found my voice.

Ariel nodded, then smiled, "Okay, well, then I'll let you rest up. Ethan told me I only had like five minutes. He like likes you, you know. Like a lot."

"I know," I said.

"Okay," Ariel said, letting go of my hand. "Bye, then."

"Bye," I said.

Ariel walked out of the room, stopping to look back at me once. Our eyes met and then she was gone. School was going to be an interesting place on Monday, that is, if I made it back there by Monday. Although, I really couldn't afford much more make-up homework, so I was actually hoping that I wouldn't have to miss much more school.

Ethan walked back into the room. My heart flipped. He was amazing.

"Hey," I said.

"Hey," Ethan grinned back. "Did it go okay with Ariel?"

"Yeah, it went great," I said, "It was so weird."

Ethan laughed, "A good weird, though, right?"

"A good weird," I said.

Ethan sat down in the chair next to me and took my hand in his. We just stared at each other in silence.

"I've been thinking," Ethan started.

"Yeah?" I asked.

"Well, it kind of feels dumb to do it like this, but how do you feel about being my girlfriend? You know, to make it official?" Ethan asked.

My jaw wanted to drop open, but I wouldn't let it. Was it possible that Ethan had been having the same thoughts regarding our status as I was? I thought guys didn't care so much about that stuff. Wait. Maybe it meant that he really, really, really like liked me. Wow. That was cool.

"Uh," I started, "Yeah, that sounds pretty cool. Sure."

I thought that was a pretty nonchalant response, especially when my brain and my heart were exploding with happiness and all I wanted to do was run around the room screaming - Ethan Ripley is officially my boyfriend! My life totally rocks!

"Cool," Ethan said.

"Cool," I said and then paused. Something else was on my mind, "Um, can I ask you a question?"

"Go for it," Ethan said.

"Can I introduce you to someone?" I asked.

"Sure," Ethan said. "But I've already met your dad."

"I know. It's not my dad," I said. "It's sort of this lady, who's kinda like my grandma and anyway, I told her about you and she really wants to meet you."

"Sure," Ethan said.

"Cool," I said.

Leonora was going to be so excited to meet Ethan and I wasn't scared what Ethan would think about that anymore. He knew me better than anyone. We had crashed funerals together. And, he like liked me enough to call me his girlfriend, no matter what anyone thought of me. Besides, Leonora really was like my grandma and I did want Ethan to meet her.

"Before we do that, though, can we plan an official date first?" Ethan asked. "I mean, our last first date, kind of ended abruptly."

Our last first one had been the Homecoming Dance and abruptly was definitely a good word for how it ended.

"I can't wait," I said. "Boyfriend."

It felt so great to say that word out loud. I wanted to shout it from the rooftops - Ethan Ripley was my boyfriend! Officially!

Ethan smiled at the word, "Good. Girlfriend."

Okay, as a note - it was even better hearing Ethan say the word girlfriend. There was only one other thing that would make this moment perfect.

"Before we do that, though..." I started.

"What?" Ethan asked.

I smiled and grabbed Ethan's shirt, pulling him toward me, and kissed him - our first official boyfriend/girlfriend kiss. Sigh. I never needed to have another peanut butter banana milkshake ever again.

ADVENTURES IN MURDER CHASING (FUNERAL CRASHING #3) SNEAK PEAK!

Ethan Ripley was my boyfriend. Officially. The first person I called and told was my ex-best friend, Ariel Walker. I knew she wouldn't be jealous, exactly, but maybe it would impress her a little. Besides, we had to make plans to meet up for peanut butter banana milkshakes.

I was even more impressed that Ariel agreed to meet me slightly less than two weeks later on a Saturday afternoon. It was prime weekend time and Ariel was making room for me in it. Of course, she did owe me her life. I had just saved it and gotten hurt doing it. I mean, I was only out of the hospital by about two weeks. So, yeah, I had taken a major risk to help my ex-bff. She should make room for me in her crowded social schedule.

I knew it probably didn't mean too much and that Ariel was probably just being grateful, but I'd take what I could get. I mean, I was kind of excited about meeting up with her. We hadn't had peanut butter banana milkshakes since our freshman year of high school. I was a junior now, so it had been at least two years since we had actually hung out as friends. I wondered what it would be like. Then the worries started. Would it be awkward and horrible? Did we have anything to talk about? Well, I had Ethan and she had Troy, but that was kind of complicated. I mean, I had gone on a date with Troy before Ariel did and she had gone after Ethan before we had started going out. So, getting into detail about them might not be a good thing. At least it was only milkshakes. Worst case, we only had to spend the time it took to drink them together.

Still, I found myself dressing to impress. I knew Ariel saw me every day at school, even though we mostly didn't talk or acknowledge each other, but I wanted to look nice for meeting up with her. She was popular and I sort of felt like I had to dress to her expectations. Of course, I didn't have tons of designer clothes, but I had at least a couple of cute tops. I had made it a point to go shopping since starting to date Ethan. I wanted to look good for him, so I was starting to exchange some of my T-shirts for cuter, sexier shirts. It was a plus then that I had something to wear to hang out with Ariel.

It took me over an hour to get ready. I don't know why exactly, but I really felt like I had to look perfect. This was important. I called Ethan on my way there. My nerves were starting to go crazy. I mean, did it mean anything that Ariel and I were having milkshakes together? Did she want to be friends again? Or, was this just Ariel's way of saying thank you for saving her life and that was it? Or, did almost dying change her view of our friendship? Like, maybe it had gone from not important to a regret or something? Maybe I was getting way ahead of myself. Maybe Ariel just wanted a peanut butter banana milkshake and I was the only other person that she knew that liked them. Yeah, my brain was totally going haywire about this whole meeting up with Ariel thing.

"Hey," Ethan said on the other end of my cellphone, interrupting my rambling train of thought.

"Hey," I said back, smiling to myself, and automatically relaxing at the sound of his voice.

I totally like liked my boyfriend. Butterflies exploded in my stomach just hearing his voice. I wished I could kiss him, but he was at his house and I was in the car. Sigh.

"You on your way?" Ethan asked.

He knew what a huge day it was in my life, "Yeah."

"Nervous?" Ethan asked.

"Totally," I said and found that I felt better simply by telling Ethan about my nerves.

"Don't be," Ethan said. "Ariel's okay. Really."

It was easy for Ethan to say. He hadn't been dropped and replaced by Ariel with new bffs freshman year like it was no big deal. Plus, Ethan was popular. Everyone liked him. He had been best friends with his friends Dave and Mike since kindergarten and he had just kept gaining more and more friends along the way. He was super lucky in the friend department. I didn't have that problem. I was known as the funeral crashing graveyard girl teen sleuth. Actually, there were probably even more colorful adjectives added into that, but I had stopped keeping track. I was who I was. My boyfriend like liked me either way. That was good enough for me.

"Do you think..." I started and then stopped, suddenly feeling nervous about asking my question out loud.

"What?" Ethan asked.

"Do you think that Ariel and I could ever be friends again? Like really?" I asked.

It had been the thought running and running through

my head ever since Ariel said she wanted to hang out. I just needed another opinion. I knew it was probably stupid, but...

Ethan paused on the other end of the line and then said, "Yes."

"Why?" I asked.

I was kind of surprised at Ethan's response. I mean, in my head I was at war because for some reason, I couldn't seem to decide what exactly I felt about Ariel regarding our friendship or lack thereof. Still, when asked the question I had just posed about me and Ariel ever being friends again, I expected most people to say: "No way!" or "Never!" or "When hell freezes over!"

"Well, you guys do have a lot in common," Ethan said, as if it was that simple.

"Like?" I asked.

I desperately tried to think of anything that Ariel and I had in common anymore. I couldn't think of one thing. Well, besides the fact that it appeared we both still liked peanut butter banana milkshakes.

"You're both stubborn," Ethan said.

"Ha, ha," I said, sarcastically.

"What? It's true," Ethan said. "And, besides that, well, you both care a lot about each other."

"What?" I asked.

Ethan had blindsided me. Ariel cared about me? What? When? In junior high? Sure. Maybe now that I had saved her life? Sure. But before? When she dumped me for a new set of friends and started making fun of me? I didn't think she cared so much about me then.

"I just think it's more complicated than you think," Ethan said. "She gets mad at you. You get mad at her. Sounds like all that getting mad at each other means that something's still there to get mad about."

Maybe Ethan was right. I had always thought it was weird that Ariel sought me out. She didn't have to. Most of the student body left me alone to do my weird graveyard girl funeral crashing stuff, but Ariel wouldn't. That was kind of interesting. Maybe a part of her missed me. That brought me to a horrifying thought. Did I miss Ariel? Yeah, I couldn't think about that.

"Are you freaking out?" Ethan asked when I had been lost in my thoughts and quiet for a full minute.

"Maybe," I hedged.

"It is just hanging out and drinking milkshakes. One step at a time," Ethan said. "No pressure. Nothing to lose, you know. And, you can call me as soon as you're done."

"Thanks," I said to Ethan.

I felt my nerves calm down a little. Okay, just one step at a time - milkshakes, first. Friendship and all that, worry about at a later date. Wow, I so like liked Ethan. He was the best boyfriend ever. He knew just what to say to make me feel better.

"You're welcome," Ethan said. I heard the strumming of his guitar.

"Are you working on your music?" I asked.

"Oh, yeah," Ethan said. "I have a tune in my head and I'm trying to work on it. I'm planning to hit the open mic at Wired next week and I want to be ready. I know it's just an open mic, but yeah, it feels important."

"I can't wait to see you perform!" I said.

"Thanks," Ethan said. "I really want the song to be perfect."

"It will be," I said. "Okay, you go work on that, then. I'm almost there anyway."

"Okay," Ethan said. "Bye then. And, call me after. I'd like to hear how it went."

I hesitated for a moment, stopping myself from saying something that I suddenly wanted to say and instead just simply said, "Yeah. Bye."

I ended the call and took a deep breath. Whoa. I had almost said the words I love you. Whoa. Double whoa. What was wrong with me? We had only been dating a few weeks and it was way too soon to say those words. I mean, I definitely like liked Ethan, but love? That was a big deal. Sure, we had been through a lot, but...whoa. It was a really, really big deal to say those words. I'd have to be careful. I mean, I didn't want to end up in one of those awkward moments where I said it and Ethan looked at me like, "Um, yeah, you're okay. I like you and stuff." That would be the worst thing ever, like mortifying beyond belief and soul crushing. I mean, I love... I mean, I like liked Ethan. Yeah, I just like liked him.

I was almost glad to arrive at Wired, so I wouldn't have a chance to think more about Ethan and the big L word. I mean, we had just become boyfriend and girlfriend. It was way too soon to be thinking about that. Right? I almost wanted to ask Ariel, but I wouldn't. I so didn't trust her not to blab my dilemma to Ethan. I mean, Ariel and I weren't rekindled bffs yet. It was just milkshakes. Right?

THE NEW GIRL WHO FOUND A DEAD
BODY
EXCERPT

Chloe sat on her luggage, watching every passing car speed by with interest, waiting for the one that was supposed to pick her up. They all seemed to weave in and out of the unending airport traffic with grace. Some even managed to stop and pick up loved ones, but her ride hadn't arrived yet. Chloe hoped that he'd be able to find her in the chaos that seemed to be LAX airport.

Chloe wondered if she'd recognize him. She hadn't seen Jake since the fifth grade, when he and his parents had moved from Illinois to California. Chloe's mother and Jake's mother had been best friends since grade school. Then they grew up and had children, only a few months apart. Thus, Chloe and Jake had been best friends as kids, always thrown into play dates when their mothers wanted to visit with each other. Then after the fifth grade, Jake and his family moved to California. Chloe and Jake had been best friends back then, but the distance and the excitement of growing up quickly made their friendship grow apart and turned it instead, into a fond childhood memory.

Chloe hadn't seen Jake since, but their mothers had still kept in constant contact. Jake's father died a couple of years before and Chloe's mother had gone back to the funeral to console her friend, coming back with stories of California and the now handsome grown-up Jake. Chloe had been more excited about hearing about California. She had already set her mind on going to California to college for film school. She had known that she was destined for California ever since the beginning of her freshman year when a girl in her class started bragging about her brother in California who made movies for a living. It sounded like the perfect life and from that moment on, Chloe had made up her mind to go to California for film school. Her parents were supportive, but money became the big issue. An out of state school would cost money and lots of it and there was no way her family could afford to send her to an out of state college. Chloe spent about half of her junior year of high school sulking with frustration at the thought of being unable to follow her dreams until her mother had approached her with an idea. She and Jake's mother had talked about it and with a year's residency in California with Jake and his mother, Chloe would be able to attend a California state school, as a resident. Chloe didn't think twice about it. She agreed. She knew she would miss her friends in Illinois, but this was a chance to follow her dream and she couldn't pass it up.

Chloe could barely believe that she was in California about to start her new life. It was all really exciting. If only Jake would show up, so she could start the adventure. Jake was supposed to meet her outside the baggage claim when she arrived, but he hadn't shown up yet. Chloe looked at her cell phone, wondering if she should call him. She felt a little shy about it. She would rather see him face-to-face first. Maybe she should text him. Why was she so scared about seeing him again?

Chloe tried to picture Jake in her mind, but could only see the little boy with unruly brown hair and mischievous blue eyes that she had played with as a child. Before she had left for California, Chloe's mother had shown her a more recent picture, but Jake had been looking at the camera with only half of his face, so Chloe wasn't quite sure what to expect when she actually saw him. Hopefully the picture her mother had sent his mother had been better. Chloe cringed inwardly, hoping that her mother hadn't sent him her last year's school picture. It had not been the best picture of her life. She had woken up late for school and hadn't had any time to make herself look good for the photo.

Looking back, Chloe realized she should have friended Jake on Facebook. It would have been a good way to get to know him again before this meeting. His profile had been set to private, though, and although, she had sat at the computer and tried to think of an email to send him or a way to add him as a friend she couldn't do it. She had just been too shy and the situation just felt too awkward. Besides, Jake hadn't sought her out either.

Chloe had tried her best to look good today, although five hours of flying had taken the curl out of her long blonde hair. She had quickly touched up her make-up before picking up her luggage, though, so she felt a little better about that. Still, she was nervous. She really wanted to make a good first impression. This was the start of the rest of her life.

"Chloe?" a male voice questioned from her right.

Chloe turned and stared into the bright blue eyes of Jake Spencer. Her breath caught and she felt her cheeks turn pink.

He was cute! He still had the unruly brown hair and his eyes had become an ocean shade of blue. A dimple creased the right corner of his mouth, making his smile contagious. Chloe smiled back.

"Hi, Jake?" Chloe said, attempting to recover from her sudden reaction to him.

"I'm so sorry! I was late and then I couldn't find you in the baggage claim and I left your cell number at home," Jake paused, catching his breath and then he grinned broadly, "It's so good to see you!"

And, before she knew it Jake was engulfing her in a hug. Chloe hugged him back and noted, with wonder, at how nice it felt to be in his arms. Chloe caught a hint of his aftershave as he pulled away.

"It's good to see you too," Chloe smiled back.

They just grinned at each other for a moment and then Jake looked away, "My girlfriend, Kate, should be here any second. She's circling, while I went to look for you. The airport's crazy."

Chloe nodded absently at his words, her mind suddenly elsewhere. Jake had a girlfriend. Of course he had a girlfriend. She felt a surge of disappointment. She immediately pushed it away. She hadn't come to California for romance. Well, she hadn't come for just romance, she admitted. Some romance would be nice eventually, but she had come for the adventure and to pursue her dream. Besides, even if it couldn't be romantic, Chloe thought, she would enjoy getting to know Jake again. It had been a long time since they had been friends and she was eager to hear about his life since then.

They stood for a few moments in silence, watching the cars fly by. Chloe felt awkward and gawky, suddenly, standing next to Jake. He was at least a head taller than her, his shoulders broad and muscular. She looked at him from the corner of her eyes as he scanned the crowd for his girlfriend. She wondered if he was still the same boy she had known in grade school. She searched his features, looking for the friend she had lost to distance so long ago.

"There she is!" Jake motioned toward a blue convertible, which screeched to a halt next to them.

Wow, Chloe thought, as the sleek car pulled up. "Is this your car?"

"Yeah," Jake grinned. "I love this car."

Chloe looked at it in admiration. It was the perfect way to arrive in California. How much more perfect than a convertible driving by the ocean could you get? Chloe felt a warm glow of happiness form in her stomach. This was going to be great!

Jake busied himself with loading her luggage into the trunk and Chloe found herself gazing awkwardly at his girlfriend, Kate. She was the epitome of the California girl – tall, blonde, with cool blue eyes, and a killer sense of fashion.

Chloe felt old fashioned in comparison despite the efforts she had made to look nice in the airport bathroom before she had gotten her luggage. Her own blonde hair was a strawberry blonde, the curls she had tried to put in that morning, falling out, and she had on the normal jeans and baby doll T-shirt that were her usual ensemble. Chloe felt almost like she was staring at a girl from a magazine, sitting inside a perfect car. Kate, on the other hand, had sleek, bleach blonde hair, make-up that looked almost professionally done, a glowing tan, a mini-skirt, and a purple lacy tank top that fit her body perfectly. Chloe had a feeling that she was going to have a lot to learn if all the girls in California looked like Kate.

"Hi, I'm Chloe," Chloe smiled, stretching out her hand.

"Kate," Kate replied dismissively, pulling on big sunglasses that hid her eyes completely.

Chloe felt her smile falter at Kate's lack of enthusiasm. She wasn't sure how to react to it.

"Okay, bags are in the trunk. Let's go!" Jake said, coming up behind Chloe.

Chloe was glad of Jake's appearance and crawled into the tiny backseat, as he sat down in the front, next to Kate. As they drove off, Chloe could almost feel Kate's cold eyes boring into her through the rear view mirror.

Chloe pushed the thought away. Perhaps Kate was a little unsettled by the thought of Chloe living with her boyfriend. When she had a chance, Chloe thought, she would reassure Kate that she had no intention of stealing Jake away from her. Chloe almost laughed at that thought. If you put her and Kate side by side, Chloe imagined, there would be no comparison. Kate would blow her out of the water in a beauty contest. Regardless, Chloe thought, she would never try and steal someone else's boyfriend, no matter how cute he had grown up to be.

As they walked up to Jake's house, Jake carrying the bulk of her luggage, Chloe couldn't help but wonder at the beauty of her new home. It was nestled into a hill above the ocean. Other houses were littered all the way down the hill, perched above blue water. The house itself was modest in size, but the exterior was cozy, almost like a chalet nested into the hill.

"Chloe!" Jeanette Spencer cried happily, seconds after Chloe walked into the house. "It's so good to see you!"

She enveloped Chloe in a hug and then stepped back

to get a better look at her, "You look just like your mom at your age! I'm so happy you're here! It'll be like having her here with me!"

Chloe grinned, "Well, you might get the real thing in about a month. She's already itching to come visit me. Thank you so much, Mrs. Spencer, for everything. "

"First of all, no Mrs. Spencer's here. Call me Jeanette. And, secondly, it's such a pleasure to have you here! I would do anything for Stacy. This will be fun," Jeanette looked over to Jake and Kate. "Do we have time for dinner or are you all off to that party?"

"Party?" Chloe looked over at Jake and managed to see a quick look pass between him and Kate. Obviously, Kate wasn't thrilled with Chloe attending the party with them. She'd have to have that talk with Kate and soon.

"We weren't sure if you wanted to go, but there's a party tonight at this girl's house on the beach, sort of a back to school thing. It's up to you, though, no pressure. I understand if you're tired from the flight and all," Jake managed, without looking at Kate again.

"Um…" Chloe felt indecisive. On the one hand, she was tired from the trip across the country, but on the other, she was absolutely energetic with excitement about her new life and a party sounded like a great way to start it all out. It would be a great way to meet the people she'd be going to school with tomorrow.

"Why are you even thinking? You're young! Go out and have a good time!" Jeanette replied before Chloe could say anything and then she looked at Jake seriously, "Just not too good of a time."

"Mom," Jake replied, laughing uncomfortably.

"What? I worry. Especially, after your father died," Jeanette's smiling face crumpled for a moment, at the memory, but then regained it's composure.

"I know," Jake said, softly.

Chloe felt uncomfortable and glanced over at Kate, who was staring at the ground.

"A party sounds perfect!" Chloe said, breaking the uneasy silence. "Let me just change clothes and I'll be ready."

Although she had forced herself to sound more cheery and energetic than she felt, Chloe really did think the party sounded fun. She picked up her backpack and swung it onto her shoulder, her mind on what she might wear to make a good impression on her new classmates, when there was a crash. She had just knocked over a vase on the kitchen table with her backpack.

"I'm so sorry!" Chloe said, automatically dropping everything and stooping down to help clean up the broken vase and flowers.

"Oh, don't worry about it!" Jeanette said, running into the kitchen for clean up supplies.

The white carnations that had looked so pretty on the kitchen table were now in a pool of water on the floor. Chloe couldn't believe she had just been so clumsy. Two minutes in their house and she had already broken something. Jake stooped down to help her, as Kate stood awkwardly nearby.

"Be careful!" Jeanette said, walking back toward them with towels and a bag for the broken glass and flowers.

As she said it, Chloe felt a piece of the vase she was collecting slice into her finger. A drop of blood escaped and stained one of the white carnations on the floor. Chloe felt a strange sense of foreboding. She should have taken the warning.

ABOUT THE AUTHOR

Milda Harris is a Chicago girl who ran off to Hollywood to pursue a screenwriting dream! She has a dog named after a piece of candy (Licorice), was once hit by a tree (seriously), and wears hot pink sunglasses (why not?). Between working in production on television shows like *Austin & Ally, Hannah Montana,* and *That's So Raven* and playing with her super cute dog Licorice, she writes young adult murder mystery, horror, paranormal romance, and chick lit novels.

Make sure to check out Milda's other books: *Adventures in Funeral Crashing (#1), Adventures in Murder Chasing (#3), The New Girl Who Found A Dead Body, Doppelganger, Doppelganger 2: On the Run,* and *Connected (A Paranormal Romance).* Funeral Crashing #4 is coming soon!

Connect online:

Website: www.mildaharris.com
Twitter: @MildaHarris
Facebook:
www.facebook.com/mildaharris

12215

Made in the USA
San Bernardino, CA
14 August 2017